THE
BR...

D0292987

HOMESTEADING in STANDING BEAR'S TERRITORY

by Bernard Palmer

A
BACK TO THE BIBLE
PUBLICATION

Back to the Bible
Lincoln, Nebraska 68501

10,000 printed to date—1976
(5-5327—10M—66)
ISBN 0-8474-6254-4

Printed in the United States of America

Contents

Chapter 1

On to Scotts Bluff

The Bradley family left home a bit earlier than usual that Sunday morning in early June and drove to the retirement center just outside of Collinsdale to pick up Grandma Redding. Eleven-year-old Trena had been given permission by her parents to invite the elderly woman to ride to Sunday school and church with them and to come home for dinner afterward. Actually, the entire family was anxious to have Mrs. Redding join them. They thought of the lonely, gray-haired widow as their grandmother and had grown to love her.

Trena was especially fond of Mrs. Redding. The red-haired girl had wanted a grandma more than anything else. So when she became acquainted with Mrs. Redding, Trena claimed her as her own grandmother and visited her at least once a week. For the past several weeks they had been reading from the old diary of Becky Prescott, Mrs. Redding's great-grandmother.

When they pulled up at the curb in front of the sprawling retirement center, nine-year-old Jon opened the station wagon door and started to get out. Trena saw what he was doing.

"I'll go get her," she said quickly, opening the door on her side.

"I'm the closest," he protested.

"But I know right where her room is."

But before either of them could get out of the station wagon, Grandma Redding appeared. They caught a glimpse of her bright shawl through the plate glass window. A moment later she scurried out the door. Clutching the huge black bag she took with her everywhere, she hurried breathlessly down the walk to the car.

"I hope I haven't kept you waiting," she said apologetically, getting in the front seat beside Mrs. Bradley.

Dr. Bradley assured her that she hadn't, explaining that they had just driven up.

"I was out in the lobby a few minutes ago," she said, "but then I remembered that I had to go back to my room for something. I guess I must be getting old. I put it out on the table the first thing this morning, so I would be sure not to forget it, but I did."

Trena smiled knowingly. "I hope it's what I think it is."

Grandma Redding turned in her seat to face the young redhead. "I'm not saying a word," she replied firmly. "Not a word. So it's not going to do you any good to ask me questions."

Jon resented the look on his sister's face. Her eyes were saying that Grandma Redding didn't have to tell her anything—she already knew what the older woman had gone back to her room to get. He didn't see why Trena got away with acting the way she did about Grandma Redding. She was his adopted grandma too! Still, he had to admit

6

there was a special bond between Grandma Redding and his older sister.

When they got home after church, 13-year-old Tim went out to finish taking care of his hens while Mrs. Bradley and Trena set the table. Five-year-old Cindy perched on Grandma Redding's lap and begged her to tell stories of the days when she was a little girl. Mrs. Redding did so, and Cindy was thrilled by them. Trena was thinking about Grandma Redding and her big purse and the thing she had gone back to her room to get, but she said nothing about it until they had finished eating and the dishes were done.

"All right, Grandma," she exclaimed, going into the living room and standing in front of her. "Where is it?"

The older woman pretended not to understand.

"You know what I'm talking about! Shall I get your purse?"

"Is there something in my purse?" Grandma Redding asked, her eyes twinkling.

"There had better be," Trena said, laughing.

"I suppose you're talking about the diary."

"That's right," the girl replied. "Is it in your purse?"

"Now, what makes you think I'd bring that diary along?" she wanted to know.

"Because you're as anxious to read the rest of it as I am!"

Mrs. Redding's face finally broke into a smile. "You're right about that. I thought we could read until we found out how the Prescotts managed after they left Fort Kearny." She was chuckling in amusement but stopped abruptly and looked around. She had just remembered the others in the room. "I'm sorry," she said. "Trena and I shouldn't be so selfish. The rest of you probably aren't interested in hearing what happened to Becky Prescott. We'll wait until another time to read it."

But Dr. Bradley and the others would not allow her to put the old diary aside. "Trena has been coming home and giving us a running account of what she's read," her father said. "We'd like to hear some of it first hand, wouldn't we, Jon?"

The younger boy nodded vigorously.

"Well," Grandma Redding said, fishing in her purse for the diary, "if you're sure you want to hear it, all right. I just didn't want to bore you."

Trena opened the diary to the place where she had stopped reading.

" 'Dear Diary,

" 'Well, I suppose you're not surprised that we're still in Fort Kearny. It was so good to see the fort and to know that we would be able to stay here for a little while. Only Pa says we've got to get moving as soon as we can. Can you believe it? It's only the first of July, and he's afraid it might snow before we get across the mountains into Oregon.

" 'He is concerned about our oxen, though. They got so skinny coming out from Independence. He wants to get them in better shape before we leave here. It's a long way to Fort Laramie, and there are only a couple of stopping places. And those are within two or three days of Fort Laramie. Pa says he's sure there won't be any oxen to buy there. He's tried to buy some around here, but there aren't any for sale. I guess we'll just have to wait.

8

" 'A small wagon train is due to leave here tomorrow. Pa would like to go with them, but we can't go so soon. Mose Skinner stopped by to see Pa this afternoon and asked us to go west with his wagon train. After the way he left us with a broken wheel on the trail east of Fort Kearny, I hope Pa tells him we won't go with him. If it hadn't been for Red Terrence and our finding Lone Wolf injured at the water hole and Standing Bear's coming to look for his foster son, I don't know what would have happened to us. Everybody said there were all sorts of war parties in that area, but Standing Bear and his men protected us. They took us almost all the way to Fort Kearny. We still thank God for him every night when we have our devotions. Pa says God sent Standing Bear to help us.' "

*   *   *

Elijah Prescott was very much concerned about going west with Mose Skinner's wagon train after what had happened before, but he was not sure he had any choice. No other wagons were going west of Fort Kearny that summer, according to the commanding officer at the fort. And he warned Elijah about attempting the trip alone, even as far as Fort Laramie.

The officer had no new information, but the last reliable report he had indicated there was Indian trouble to the west. Stories came to him of war parties being seen along the trail and of horses being stolen. He was not sure there was any truth to what he had heard, but he was inclined to believe that the Sioux were about to hit the warpath.

He linked Standing Bear with the uprisings. When Elijah expressed his own disbelief, the colonel bristled.

"Don't you think he wouldn't be behind this kind of turmoil. He'd kill women and children or anyone else who stood in his way. That old scoundrel would take his grandmother's scalp if he thought it would keep the whites from goin' across the prairies. I've been in these parts off and on for seven years, Prescott, and let me tell you somethin'. I wouldn't put nothin' past that character!"

Elijah was still unconvinced, but he did not press the argument. It was then that he decided to accept Mose Skinner's offer to go west with his group. Elijah had been prayerfully considering the matter ever since the rough wagon master had sought him out and talked with him about it several days before. He had not changed his opinion of the man, but the more he prayed, the more positive he was that going with Mose was the only course open to them.

Actually, it was very much as Red Terrence had said, and Red knew Mose Skinner better than most people did. He had traveled with him long enough to be aware of his strengths and his shortcomings. Mose was a hard man and not very likeable, but he had been born and raised in the West. He knew the country better than most of the scouts on the trail, and although he hated them, he knew the Indians too. Red always said that if anyone could get a wagon train through, it was Skinner.

Elijah was well aware that his family would not be pleased with his decision. Thirteen-year-old Samuel had already expressed himself, and the bearded settler was sure his wife and daughter would agree with his son. He was not surprised when his wife voiced her opposition.

"I don't see why we're goin' to take a chance on that Mose Skinner again," Hannah protested. "You know what he did to us the last time."

"Yes," Elijah answered quietly, "I know what he did, but we don't have any choice. It's either go on west with the train he's leadin' or winter right here at Fort Kearny. I've checked into it, Hannah. There's not goin' to be any other train west till spring."

Concern showed in her tired eyes, but she remained silent.

"I've been askin' God to guide us," he told her. "I haven't made the decision on my own."

She put her hand on his arm tenderly. "I know that, Elijah," she said. "You always do seek the mind of the Lord before you make a hard decision. I'm sorry I said anything. If you feel it's best for us to go with Skinner, I'm not wantin' to tell you what we should do."

They ate around the campfire that night and had a long time of prayer, asking God to guide them safely across the prairies and to protect and care for Mose Skinner and all the others who would be traveling with him. When they finished praying, Red Terrence was grinning broadly.

"What's got into you?" Becky asked him.

"I was just wonderin' what old Mose would think if he could have heard me prayin' for him just now."

11

"He'd probably thank you for it," she replied. "Most people like to have someone pray for them."

"Not Mose! He'd blow up for sure if he knew it."

Elijah was silent for a time. "Have you ever let him know that you're a Christian now?"

"I sure haven't!" he exclaimed. "And I don't plan on it, either."

"Did you know that the Bible says something about that, Red?" the settler asked. "If we don't let people know that we're believers, it's the same as denyin' the Lord Jesus. And if we deny Him before men, He'll deny us before God."

Red's face paled, causing his freckles to stand out like so many buffalo against the hills. "What's a guy supposed to do?"

"We're supposed to let people know where we stand."

"It sure won't be easy," Red replied, his lips trembling.

"I'm sure it won't be."

"But we'll all be prayin' for you, won't we, Pa," Becky put in quickly.

"That we will," Elijah said, grinning at his 11-year-old daughter. "That we will, Becky."

The day before the wagon train was to leave, Elijah talked with the colonel once more. A patrol had just returned, he said, with encouraging news. The Indian trouble that had been so disturbing in recent weeks seemed to have subsided. There were few signs of any Indians, even hunting parties, west of Fort Kearny, and it sounded as though Standing Bear had suddenly packed up and headed to the northwest with his tribe. At least that was the

12

information an old mountain man on the trail gave the patrol. As far as the colonel was concerned, that was always good news. Anytime the sly chief was close, it spelled big trouble.

The following morning the wagon train headed west toward Fort Laramie and Oregon. The settlers traveling with Skinner were entirely different than they had been when they left Independence earlier in the season. Then, it had taken hours for them to get their wagons moving. And every morning had been the same—they jostled and fumbled about as they yoked their oxen and got their wagons into position.

Now they were as disciplined and as hardened as army troops. With a minimum of delay and confusion the train formed and inched west out of Fort Kearny. Dust spiraled up from the hooves of the oxen, horses and cattle with every step and clung to their hides. The sun pounded mercilessly on the wagons, travelers and animals as they trudged along the trail.

Becky thought the first day out of Fort Kearny would never end. In the morning she walked and ran beside the wagon, thankful to be on the move once more. But as the sun moved higher in the sky, she felt the heat beating down on her. By mid-afternoon she climbed into the wagon and lay down for awhile. When they finally stopped to make camp, she was so tired she didn't think she could even eat supper.

The next three days were repetitions of the first. What had been exciting to her when they left Fort Kearny soon became drab and wearing. She was beginning to wonder if they would ever get to Fort Laramie, let alone to Oregon.

Samuel Prescott and Red Terrence were busy with the wagons all day, but at night, after they had finished their chores and had supper, they gathered with the scouts. In spite of the fact that the army had been unable to find any trace of Indians, the scouts were concerned. It was true that there were no big bands around and few signs, but there was evidence that Indians were nearby. They occasionally saw unshod hoofprints near the water holes, and sometimes a signal fire sent up its thin spiral of smoke, stark and ominous against the pale summer sky.

"I don't like it," Red told Samuel and Elijah. "You know there are Indians around here. There must be! They've been everywhere else we've been on this trip. It just doesn't stand to reason that they'd vanish all of a sudden."

"Maybe the buffalo have drifted to places where there's more grass," Elijah countered. "If that's the case, the Indians would follow them."

The boy nodded doubtfully. "Maybe," he said. "And maybe not. When Indian signs seem to disappear, that's when you've got to double the guard. They can cross ten miles of wet sand without leavin' a track if they want to."

As far as Samuel was concerned, Red's uneasiness was catching. He found himself searching the skies for the telltale wisps of smoke signals and the hills for a fleeting glimpse of an Indian scout watching the course of the wagon train. However, they did not meet any hostile Indians, although they did see several small bands of braves. The Indians seemed to be traveling fast and acted as though they did not want trouble. At least they kept their distance from the wagon train.

The settlers did not have any difficulty on this part of the trip—not even a broken wheel. The trip was uneventful all the way to Chimney Rock and Scotts Bluff.

"We've been makin' good time," Elijah told his family the evening they reached Scotts Bluff. "From what I understand, when we get to Fort Laramie, we'll have passed the half-way mark on our trip from Illinois to Oregon."

"It's a long way to Oregon," Red said. "And we've still got the worst of the trip ahead of us. Goin' over those mountains is rough!"

They were still having their devotions that evening when they were interrupted by a flurry of activity not far from their wagon. Elijah stopped reading the Bible at the first sound of excited voices.

"What's goin' on out there?" Samuel asked nervously.

"Why don't you go and see?" his father said.

Obediently he got to his feet and left the wagon. A dozen or more people were gathered in an excited little circle around the two riders. Two men were standing on the fringe, talking, when Samuel came running up.

"What's going on?" Samuel asked them.

"The scouts brought somebody back with them," one of the men said.

"Somethin' wrong?"

"That's what we came to find out," the other said.

Chapter 2

A Stranger's Gold Dust

Samuel Prescott turned from the men and pushed through the excited crowd so he could see the scout and the newcomer. The boy stared at the wizened little man in worn buckskin. There were a thousand unanswered questions in Samuel's eyes.

"I want you all to meet Jake Gaudine," the scout said, indicating his companion. "I found him over the ridge on the other side of the river. He was leadin' a lame horse."

"And it's a mighty good thing you came along when you did too," Jake exclaimed. "I don't mind tellin' you, I was gettin' tuckered out. Didn't know how long I'd be able to keep goin'."

"See any Indians out there?" one of the men called out.

He grinned crookedly. "Still got my hair, don't I?"

The people had other questions. They wanted to know which direction he came from and how long he'd been on the trail and what it was like up ahead. He answered them frankly but would not tell them where he had come from. He had been on the trail for a couple of weeks, he guessed. He had sort of lost track of time. The trail was good as far as Fort Laramie, but after that the going got tough.

"Where'd you come from?" someone asked again.

Gaudine's eyes squinted narrowly. "I'm from Boston," he said pointedly. "Where're you from?"

"That's not what I meant."

"I know it's not," he snapped. Then, deliberately, he turned to the scout who had brought him in. "You know, I'm gettin' mighty hungry."

"I'll bet you are, at that," the scout answered. "Come with me, and we'll see if we can rustle up some grub." As he spoke, his gaze met Samuel's. He was one of the men Red and Samuel visited almost every night after their work was done. "Your ma's a good cook. Think she'd be able to get our starvin' friend somethin' to eat?"

"Sure she would. Come on over to our campfire."

The stranger hesitated. "That's right neighborly of you, but maybe you'd better go ask your ma first. She might not want company tonight."

"That won't make any difference," Samuel told him. "She's always got food for someone who's hungry."

When Samuel returned to the campfire with the two men, Elijah invited them to sit down. "We're just finishin' our devotions for the evenin'," he said. "As soon as we have our prayer, we'll see what we can do about gettin' you somethin' to eat."

The men squatted uncomfortably on the ground across the campfire from Elijah and his family, as far away as possible. Their presence did not change the Prescotts' regular habit of praying, however. It was Elijah's turn to lead that evening. He asked each one to name things they should pray about, then each took his turn in thanking God for watching over them and asking Him to keep them safe from harm.

Having the scout and Jake Gaudine present bothered Red as much as it bothered them. When it was his turn to voice a prayer request, he mumbled so much that Elijah had to ask him to repeat what he had said. At last he looked directly at the older man, his face as fiery red as his hair.

"I said we should pray that we'll get to Fort Laramie safely," he muttered.

Gaudine snickered and punched his companion in the ribs. "I should've had you out on the trail with me to pray that my horse wouldn't go lame. I could've been where I was goin' by now."

Becky's eyes blazed. She didn't like having anyone make fun of Red, especially about his new love for Jesus Christ.

"It would've helped," she said seriously. "It would even have helped if you'd prayed." She paused. "That is if you've admitted you're a sinner and put your trust in Jesus Christ to save you."

For almost a minute a tense silence gripped the little knot of people around the campfire. Then the scout laughed scornfully. "That should hold you, Gaudine," he retorted.

"I think we've had quite enough of that kind of talk," Elijah said quietly but in a way that was not to be ignored. "We don't ridicule anyone about his faith or his lack of it. It's far too serious for that."

When it was Becky's turn to pray, she asked God to work in Jake Gaudine's heart, making him

19

realize that he was a sinner and would go to hell unless he trusted Christ to save him. A long silence followed the last prayer, which was Elijah's. The two men got to their feet and would have left had it not been for Hannah.

"I'll have somethin' for you to eat right away," she said, "as soon as we get the fire built up a little more."

Samuel went for some buffalo chips, and in a few minutes Mrs. Prescott had finished frying some meat and making coffee for their guests. While they ate, Gaudine asked if they knew where he could get another horse.

"I'd be willin' to leave my buckskin for free and pay twice the goin' price for a good horse." He reached into his shirt pocket and took out a leather pouch. "And I'll pay in gold dust!"

Samuel caught his breath. The only people who had gold dust were those who had made a strike or had robbed somebody else who had found gold.

"I'm afraid you'll have a hard time gettin' a horse for any price from anyone in the wagon train," Elijah told him.

Gaudine's eyes narrowed. "I'd be willin' to pay four times what a horse is worth," he said.

"I still don't think you could buy one." He turned to the scout who had found the mountain man in the hills. "What do you think about it?" he asked.

"I've got to agree with you, Elijah." He didn't think Jake would be able to buy a horse, regardless of what he was willing to pay.

"I sure wouldn't want to have to steal one," Gaudine said. "I've never stolen anything in my whole life."

"There has to be some other way of gettin' where you want to go," Red put in. "Ways that'd be a heap safer than horse stealin'. Around here, they hang men for that."

The mountain man's face darkened. "I've been around these parts since before you were born. You can't tell me anythin' I don't know already. But I'm goin' to get where I'm goin'. I don't want to steal a horse, but I might have to! Don't think I won't, if it comes to that! I've got a fortune waitin' for me, and no lame saddle bronc is goin' to keep me from gettin' it."

The air was electric for a moment or two.

*   *   *

Samuel Prescott didn't know how the story of Jake Gaudine and his gold dust got out. He had said nothing to anyone about it, and he was sure Red and the rest of the family had kept silent about the stranger and his secret. The following morning, however, everyone knew about it. Two or three boys Samuel's age knew the mountain man had eaten with them the night before and asked about him. They wanted to know if he had said anything about where he made his strike or how soon he was going back to work it.

They seemed to know more about it than Samuel did. They wondered if he had said whether he had been to the Black Hills or to the mountains of Wyoming and wanted to know if he had been working his claim for long. When the Prescott boy said he didn't know anything about it, they acted as though he was lying to them.

"All I know about it," he said, "is that Mr. Gaudine wanted to buy a horse from us and offered to pay us in gold dust."

"He was over to see us too," one of the others replied. "He even offered to throw in that buckskin of his. Said he'd be as good as new in a couple of weeks or so."

"My pa said for two cents he'd forget about goin' on to Oregon," one of the others said excitedly. "He figures it doesn't make sense to be a dirt farmer if a man's got a chance to strike it rich with a gold claim."

That night two of the scouts who had left Independence with the wagon train took off without even collecting their pay. Red came back to the wagon with the story.

"Why would they do that, Pa?" Samuel wanted to know.

Elijah put an arm around his son's shoulder affectionately. "The prospect of hunting for gold does some strange things to men."

When they stopped to eat at noon, Mose Skinner came riding up to talk to Mr. Prescott. He wanted to know if Gaudine had said anything about where he'd made his strike. All Elijah could tell him was that the mountain man fished a pouch from his pocket and let him hold it in his hand. It was mighty heavy, the settler said. Heavier than anything else of that size he'd ever held.

Mose swore. "That's what everybody on this whole wagon train says. The two best scouts we've got took off last night, and the way the others are talkin', I don't know how many'll even be with us as far as Fort Laramie."

It was something they had to be much in

prayer about, Elijah explained to his family at supper that night. The fact that the mountain man was still eating with them made no difference. He asked Hannah to lead them in Bible reading and prayer.

"And be sure to remember the problem we've got with the scouts who are leadin' us out to Oregon," he said. "Ask God to keep them from goin' off tryin' to find gold."

Jake squirmed uncomfortably as she prayed, and as soon as she had finished, he coughed nervously and got to his feet.

"I'll be seein' you," he mumbled. "I've got somethin' to do."

The following evening, an hour or so before sundown, the little wagon train pulled into Fort Laramie. Skinner passed the word to the wagon owners that they would not be staying there long.

"It's the 15th of July now," he said, "and we've still got a long way to go. If we're goin' to make it across the mountains before the snow blocks the passes, we're goin' to have to get movin'. So if you've got anything to do here that has to be done, you'd better get with it!"

Actually, there was little need for the announcement. The men all knew that time was getting away from them. They would have to be moving on soon if they were to make it across the mountain passes before the snow blocked them. The group bustled about, trying to get everything done in the short time they had. Elijah had some supplies to get, and Samuel was sent to the blacksmith to get new horseshoes for his saddle pony. Red decided to do the same. While they were at the shop, the blacksmith asked them about the wagon train and especially about the story of the gold strike.

"Everybody's talkin' about it," he said. "I hear that two more scouts took off today."

Samuel and Red tried not to show their concern, but as soon as the blacksmith finished with their horses, they went back to the wagon and told Elijah. He did not seem to be surprised.

"Mose went by here a few minutes ago," he said. "He's callin' another meetin' of the men tonight. Said it was very important."

"Do you suppose he wants to tell us about losin' two more scouts?" Red asked.

"Could be," Elijah answered. Actually, however, he was sure it was much more than that. Mose had lost men before without getting upset about it. They weren't out on the trail; they were in Fort Laramie where they should be able to pick up plenty of replacements.

Shortly after sundown the little group gathered. It was obvious that the men expected more than an announcement about the two scouts who had just quit their jobs. There was little conversation as they came together.

Mose Skinner got to his feet when they were all assembled and raised his voice. "We've got ourselves a problem," he began. "And in all the years I've been out here takin' wagons across the prairies, I've never faced anything like this before. We've got to decide whether we go on or not."

"Is it that serious?" someone called out.

"It's that serious!"

24

Chapter 3

Decision at Fort Laramie

Concern and dismay rippled through the crowd of men. Most of them were in the same situation as Elijah Prescott. It had taken most of their money to buy wagons and oxen and to travel as far as they had come already. They would have enough to get to Oregon, with a little left over for seed and supplies, but wintering at Fort Laramie was something they had not planned on. It would leave them with serious financial problems.

Mose Skinner went on to explain why he thought they should consider staying at the Army fort. They had gotten a late start out of Independence in the spring and had been delayed longer than usual in Fort Kearny while waiting for their oxen and horses to get rested and back into shape for the journey west. They were in good shape now—at least it seemed that way to him—but time was against them. They should have left Fort Laramie at least two weeks earlier.

And they still couldn't leave yet or even make plans to leave. They were short four scouts and would have to find recruits before they could even consider going on. And finding help in a place like Fort Laramie wasn't going to be easy, especially with the outbreak of gold fever that had robbed him of four good men and had taken at least a dozen others, not including three soldiers who had deserted to search for gold.

"I don't mind tellin' you," Mose went on, "that we're in plenty of trouble. I've spent the day tryin' to find replacements for the men we've lost, but I haven't been able to get a single one. If they haven't already set out to hunt for gold, they're fixin' to. It looks to me as if we're in for plenty of trouble if we think about goin' on. I'd like to suggest we winter here. Come spring the gold seekers'll come sneakin' back here, worn out and flat broke. They'll be beggin' for work, and we'll have the whole summer to get across the mountains."

"Only most of us don't have enough money to hole up here for the winter," one of the settlers said. "That's my problem."

"Mine too," another echoed. "How about it, Skinner? Would you take us on to Oregon this year if we agree to do the scoutin' for you?"

Mose Skinner was silent for a time. "I reckon so, if you're willin' to risk it. But I'm tellin' you right now, we've got a job on our hands. It's goin' to make what we've been through the past few weeks seem like a walk home from church in the summertime."

Several of the men asked questions about the Indians and what they could expect from them during the rest of the trip. Others were more concerned about the mountains they would be crossing over and the rivers they would have to ford. Finally, after a great deal of discussion, they

26

decided to take a vote. As Skinner called out each man's name, he told whether he wanted to go on under those conditions or remain in Fort Laramie for the winter. Most decided to continue, but four voted to stay at the Army fort. Skinner was deeply disturbed.

He didn't know what he should do, he told Elijah, who was sitting near him. There weren't many men to start with. They had lost four scouts, and now four wagons were going to remain behind. That didn't leave them with enough men to be sure they could keep the wagons moving and still do a decent job of scouting for hostile Indians.

"I'm goin' to get everybody together tomorrow night," he announced. "We'll take another vote, and if it's the same, we'll consider disbanding the wagon train, at least 'til the winter's over."

"Does that mean we'll have to stay here whether we want to or not?" one of them asked.

"That's about the size of it. I'm not leavin' here unless I'm sure we've got enough men along to get us safely over the mountains to Oregon. So be thinkin' about it and talkin' among yourselves. Oh, and if you want to do any prayin', that might not be a bad idea." He pulled in a deep breath. "All right, the meeting's over." He jerked his hat lower over his eyes and stomped away.

Elijah turned to Samuel and Red Terrence. "Let's get ourselves back to the wagon," he said. "We've got a lot of prayin' to do."

Red Terrence glanced over his shoulder at Mose, who had been stopped by a couple of settlers. For some reason the wagon master's casual statement about praying had set his heart aflame.

27

He wanted to go right over there, grab Skinner by the shirt collar and tell him he was a Christian now and would be praying about whether the wagon train should go on that summer or not. He stopped walking and half turned to go back to the place where the wagon master was standing, but even thinking about telling Mose Skinner that he was a Christian made his heart hammer and his tongue swell.

Samuel stopped. "Hey, Red!" he called out. "Are you comin'?"

At first the youthful scout did not reply. The settler's son repeated the question.

"Me?" Red echoed. "Oh, sure. Sure, I'm comin'." He hurried to catch up with his companions.

"I thought maybe you were goin' to do somethin' else," Samuel told him.

Red hesitated. He could not lie about it, but he didn't want to say anything to Elijah and his son—at least not right then. "I was," he replied, "but I—I decided to forget it, at least for tonight."

"Think it would do any good to go and ask Mose Skinner to change his mind?" Samuel wanted to know.

"I don't reckon that'd be wise," Elijah countered. "It's like Red says. Mose Skinner knows this trail as well as a dirt farmer back home knows his fields. If he thought it'd be safe for us to go on with the men we'd have on the wagon train, he'd never even ask us to vote on it again. He'd tell us we were leavin' on such and such a day, and that'd be the end of it."

The next morning Elijah and Samuel went to see a couple of the men who had voted against

28

going on to Oregon that summer. When they came back, Mr. Prescott was deeply disturbed. The men were not afraid to go on, but they had decided to leave their families at Fort Laramie and go to the Black Hills in an effort to find gold themselves. Elijah tried to talk them out of it, but they had already made up their minds.

They weren't the only ones, they said. Others who were wavering had decided that they, too, would take advantage of the time at Fort Laramie to join the gold rush.

The Prescotts were not considering the gold rush, but they were disturbed about the way things were working out.

"I can't understand it," Elijah told Hannah and the others. "God's leading west was so plain to all of us, but now I don't know what He would have us to do. We've asked Him to show us His will, but there isn't any answer. We don't have any peace in the matter."

"Don't you think He's showin' us that we shouldn't go on to Oregon until spring?" Hannah asked.

"Or," Mr. Prescott said thoughtfully, "maybe He's showing us that He doesn't want us to go on to Oregon at all."

"Why would He do that?" Samuel asked.

"I don't rightly know, but I've been doin' a lot of thinkin' about it the past couple of days or so. It could be that He used Oregon to get us out of where we were. Now that we're on the trail, God may be showin' us what He really wants for us."

The rest of the family eyed Elijah questioningly.

29

"What have you been thinkin' God might want us to do?" his wife asked.

He held out his cup, and she filled it with scalding coffee. "There's only one thing I can think of," he said, "and I know it doesn't make too much sense. Do you suppose God wants us to settle along here some place?"

Anguish leaped to Hannah's face. "You can't be serious, Elijah!"

"I don't know that He wants us to do that. I'm just thinkin' out loud."

"You don't know what you're sayin', Elijah," Red Terrence broke in. "This country's rough! No tribe of Indians, except the Apache, is half as warlike as the Sioux. They'd have our scalps before Christmas."

Becky Prescott shuddered, and her mother's cheeks paled, but neither of them spoke.

"God has given us a real opening with Standing Bear and Lone Wolf," Mr. Prescott continued. "Maybe He wants us to stay around here where we might have a chance to reach some of Standing Bear's people for Christ—maybe even the chief himself. If He's leadin' us that way, Red, He'll take care of us. I don't have any fear about that."

Red nodded. He was a believer, too, but he didn't see how Elijah could be so convinced that God would take care of them. He knew all too well what Standing Bear and the other Sioux war chiefs in the territory were like.

He didn't know why he happened to think about the area northeast of Fort Laramie or why he even mentioned it. He certainly didn't think the settler would be interested in going there. But he remembered hearing about it from a cowboy who had herded cattle up from the big state of Texas.

"You could go into the bluestem area," he said. "That is, if you aren't afraid to go into a place where I've heard the Indians are afraid to go more than a mile or two. All sorts of stray mavericks are roaming in that area. There're men who've quit the trail and have gone there with a rope to build up a herd of their own."

"Wouldn't that be stealing?" Becky asked.

"Not so anybody could notice. The men movin' the herds have got too much to do to go wanderin' around tryin' to find strays. Besides, I think a lot of 'em are half afraid to leave the trail."

Elijah had a thousand questions about the area northeast of Fort Laramie. He questioned Red at length about the Indians and why they were afraid to go into the vast area. He also asked if there were any settlers there.

"The only ones I ever heard of were the ranchers I was tellin' you about," Red replied. "And I don't think there're too many of them. Then there's the new fort that's been built up there somewhere."

"You mean Fort Robinson?"

The youthful scout nodded. "That's right. I don't know how many soldiers they've got up there, but it must be about like Fort Laramie."

Elijah frowned and tugged thoughtfully at the lobe of his ear. "Now, that would be an advantage. We might be able to go up there close to the fort. There'd be some protection, and it won't be long 'til there'll be other settlers goin' in to live."

Becky was dismayed to think about living in a place like that. She wasn't superstitious, as the

31

Indians apparently were, but it did bother her. She wondered why the Indian people would be afraid to go there. Maybe wild animals lived there that weren't found in any other part of the Great Plains, or maybe there was some other reason they didn't tell about.

"Does—does that mean we're goin' to settle there, Pa?" she asked, her voice quavering.

His smile was gentle. "No, Becky, it doesn't. We're still seekin' the will of the Lord. It's somethin' we're supposed to be prayin' about. We can't make up our minds right now."

Even though it wasn't time yet for evening devotions, they spent a long time in prayer.

Right after their noon meal Elijah took his son and Red with him to see the commanding officer of Fort Laramie. The colonel was friendly but quite discouraging.

"I don't have any right to keep you out of there, Mr. Prescott," he said. "This is a free country, and a man can do as he pleases, but I can tell you the area is considered to be very dangerous."

"Even with the new fort?"

"That could make a difference. On the other hand, Standing Bear and his tribe have moved into that area now, and he is one Indian nobody dares to fool with."

Elijah started to tell him that he knew the Indian chief to be an entirely different type of person, but he checked himself. It wouldn't do any good. The officer had already made up his mind about Standing Bear. He wouldn't want to hear what anyone else had to say about the Indian.

"What would you think if we decided to go up there and have a look?"

The army officer got to his feet and came around to the other side of the desk. "I'd think you were mighty determined people—and mighty reckless!"

Chapter 4

The Scouting Trip

At the meeting that evening Mose again asked for a vote on what the wagon train should do.

"Well, I'm afraid that settles it," he said when it became apparent that none of the men had changed their minds. "It just isn't safe to try to make it without more help. We'll have to spend the winter here."

For the next several days Elijah talked about settling in the area northeast of Fort Laramie. Taking Red and Samuel with him, he went to see anyone who had been there or knew anything about the area. Some expressed concern about the superstitions and fears of the Indian people regarding that section of the territory. There had to be some reason for their fears besides the spirits the Indians believed lived there, they said. Others laughed at the myths that were told about the grass-covered hills. But on one thing they all agreed. It was a fabulous land with rich soil and an abundance of game. Finally, Elijah decided to go and take a look at it.

"It isn't good to go to a place like that to live unless we've seen it ourselves," Elijah announced to the family. "But I've been prayin' about it and

35

talkin' to everyone I can find who's ever been there. I believe we ought to go and see it for ourselves."

"Can I go along?" Samuel asked.

His pa did not answer him right away. "I'll have to see about that," he said. "We might need you to look after things back here."

The boy could not hide his disappointment, but he did not argue with his father. If his pa wanted him to stay and take care of the oxen, that's what he would do without complaint. Besides, it did no good to protest. If his pa said something, that was the way it would be. Talk wouldn't get him to change his mind.

There was a certain amount of last-minute work to be done before Elijah and Red left Fort Laramie, and Red and Samuel were kept busy helping to get things ready. Shortly after noon they went to the trading post for a few supplies they still needed. They were on their way back to the wagons when Mose Skinner approached.

"What's this I hear about Elijah goin' to settle in the bluestem, Red?" he asked.

"We're goin' to look it over, but he hasn't decided anything more than that."

Skinner's eyes narrowed questioningly. "You know old Standing Bear's roamin' around those parts, don't you? He's the only chief who's not afraid to go in there. He's not afraid of anything!"

Red Terrence hesitated. He had been praying and praying that God would give him the opportunity and the courage to tell the wagon master about his newfound faith, but just thinking about it brought sweat to his forehead.

"Pa isn't scared of Standing Bear," Samuel put in. "He's a friend of ours."

Mose snorted in scorn. "That old scoundrel's never had a white friend. He might act like it, but that's just to get you off your guard. I'm warnin' you. And if you're smart, you'll tell your pa what I say. If you trust Standing Bear, he'll slit your throats some day or lift that hair of yours. And all the prayin' you do won't help a bit." He glanced at Red. "Isn't that right, Red?"

The youthful scout swallowed hard. He had asked God to give him a chance to tell his former boss about his new faith in Jesus Christ. Now he had it, and the words stuck in his throat.

"Isn't that right, Red?" Mose repeated.

The boy pulled in a deep breath. "C—Can't say as it is, Mose," he stammered. "I—I've seen a lot of things change because of prayer."

The wagon master was surprised and showed it in his hard face. "You sound like one of those prayin' kind, Terrence."

"Maybe I am."

Skinner's voice was mocking. "I never figured that'd happen. This's somethin' I gotta see. Why don't you get down on your knees and show me how it's done. OK?"

Red's cheeks were scarlet. "I don't know of anyone who needs prayer more than you do, Mose," he blurted. He was about to say more, but the wagon master cut in abruptly.

"I do. If you go into that rough country, you'd better save those prayers of yours. You'll need 'em."

He left before Red had an opportunity to reply.

Both Samuel and his older companion were silent the rest of the way back to the wagon. Red didn't know what was the matter with him. He had wanted to tell Mose about his new faith and had even laid awake at night planning just what he would say. As Mrs. Prescott suggested, he had been praying that God would give him a chance to talk to Mose.

But when the opening came, what happened? He made a remark that was more antagonizing than anything else. He had let him know he was a Christian; at least he thought he had. But that was all. What he said sure wouldn't have made Mose want to become a believer too. He was quiet and uneasy for the rest of the afternoon.

Samuel had given up the idea of going with his pa and Red, but when they had finished their devotions after supper, Elijah informed him that he could go along.

"I've talked it over with your ma," he said quietly, "and we decided she and Becky can take care of the stock for a few days."

The boy's eyes widened, and at first he had difficulty speaking. "You—you mean I can go along?" he echoed, as though he had to have confirmation to be sure he had heard correctly.

Elijah glanced at Red and winked. "Or maybe you'd rather stay here?"

"Oh, no! I want to go along, Pa." He got to his feet. "Maybe I'd better be gettin' my gear together."

Their prayers that night were for their safety on the trip and for wisdom as they looked over the area.

The following morning they were up long

before dawn. As soon as they had eaten breakfast, they saddled their horses and headed northeast. By the time the sun came up, the trio was out of sight of the fort. Everywhere they looked there was a vast, empty stretch of prairie, unbroken by even a trail.

Samuel hoped Red would be able to guide them safely to the area they were considering for their new home and back again. Red acted confident enough, but it did make a person feel uneasy. As far as he could see in any direction were prairies and hills, without a single landmark to show them they were traveling in the right direction. Samuel shivered and tried to shove the thought aside.

They were traveling much faster than a wagon train would have. By noon they had covered more ground than Mose Skinner could have hoped to cover in a long day.

In spite of the uneasiness that gripped Samuel Prescott at times, he enjoyed riding through the hills. It seemed good not to have anything to think about except his own horse. Their only other concern was the fact that Indians were around. They had been seeing signs of them since it was light enough for them to make out hoofprints and old campfires. He would be glad when they got into the bluestem area. When they got there, they wouldn't have to worry about any Indians except Standing Bear and his warriors. Samuel still could not believe they had to be afraid of their Indian friend.

It was midafternoon, and they were plodding sleepily over the hills when Samuel suddenly saw movement ahead. It was brief and fleeting, a dark flicker of shadow against the prairie half the distance to the horizon. Ordinarily he would have thought nothing about it, but after talking to Mose Skinner and hearing what the commanding officer told his pa, a quick spasm of fear gripped him. He reined in, his gaze searching the valley ahead.

"Come on, Samuel," his father said impatiently. "We've got a long way to go. We can't be foolin' around, or we'll never get there."

Still the boy did not move. "What's that, Red?" he asked.

The youthful scout stared in the direction Samuel was pointing but could see nothing. Neither could Elijah, who was usually keen eyed and observant.

"You must be mistaken," his pa told him.

"I—I saw something," he said hesitantly. "I swear it."

"Maybe it was a coyote. They can look awfully big sometimes."

The boy remained silent, his eyes still trying to sort out the object he had seen a few moments before. His pa and Red were so insistent that he had seen nothing, he was beginning to wonder if he had been mistaken. Or perhaps he was so worried about seeing Indians on the warpath that he was trying to make something threatening out of every coyote or bunch of sagebrush on the prairie.

"You might be right," he acknowledged reluctantly, "but I sure thought I—" The words choked in his throat. There it was again! This time he got a little longer look. Whatever it was, they were closer by now, and the shadow stayed in view for several seconds. "Look!" he cried out impulsively. His hand trembled as he pointed.

40

This time Red and Elijah both saw the shadow. While they looked, the shadow disappeared, but in a half minute or so it came into view again. A tremor ran through Samuel. There was no mistaking it this time! Something was ahead! And they didn't need to be any closer to tell what that something was! There were men on horseback! And they were riding directly toward them.

"It could be a detachment of solders from Fort Robinson," Elijah said hesitantly, as though he really didn't believe it but was trying to make himself think it was true.

Red Terrence shook his head. "They're not soldiers," he countered. "I'd bet my last dollar on that. Whoever it is, they don't look like soldiers the way they sit on their horses."

"Who do you think it is?" Elijah demanded.

"Well, there's one thing I can tell you," Red continued. "They're not white men!"

Fear clutched Samuel and squeezed him dry of emotion. If they were Indians, it was either a hunting party or—or hostiles! There was no other explanation. And they had come across little sign of game, which would tend to rule out a hunting party.

While they watched, the figures on the other side of the valley disappeared.

"We'd better head toward the river," Red Terrence said breathlessly. "If that's a war party, and I've got a hunch it is, we'll have a better chance of stayin' out of trouble if we're in those willows."

Samuel knew that what his young friend said was true. He had listened to enough talk on the trail to know that an Indian war party would seldom go into the trees after anyone. They were too wary to put themselves in a position where the other side would have a chance to get off the first shot. So going to the trees along the river was the best move they could make.

They kicked their mounts in the flanks and headed for the stream at a fast gallop. But they were not fast enough. Or the war party was moving much faster than they were. They charged over a little rise and came face to face with half a dozen Indian braves, not more than 400 yards away! Briefly, both groups were so startled they jerked their horses to a halt and stared at each other, remaining motionless. Then a wild, chilling shriek of combat split the stifling summer air.

"Come on!" Red shouted. They wheeled their horses and began to race at a desperate gallop over the rough terrain in the direction of the willow trees along the river. Kicking their horses with every stride, they were soon hurtling at top speed in a mad dash for safety.

One of the warriors shot his rifle. They were out of range, although that would have made little difference. Riding at such a pace, the brave was not too accurate in his aim. Still, the report sent chills through Samuel and his companions. The boy leaned forward on his wiry little mare, pressing his body close against her and urging her on.

He didn't know she could run so hard—she never had before. She seemed to sense the critical situation and responded with every muscle, stretching out until her belly almost touched the ground.

Red's buckskin and Elijah's powerful gray were running the same way, giving all they had in a frantic attempt to lengthen the distance between them and their pursuers.

Another rifle sounded. It sounded so much farther back that Samuel risked a quick look. They were gaining on the war party, putting precious extra yards between themselves and the hostiles. The brief reprieve caused him to urge his saddle pony forward without slacking off.

Another brief, agonizing minute and they were in the willows. The instant they were screened from the view of their pursuers, Red jerked his horse to a halt and leaped off, his rifle in his hand.

''What're we goin' to do now?'' Samuel demanded. ''Do you think they'll come in after us?''

''Not likely.'' His breath was coming in great, laborious gasps. ''They're too smart for that! You're not likely to find an Indian going into an area like this in pursuit where the enemy has a good chance of getting off the first shot.'' He paused for an instant. ''They know the white man's too good with his rifle to risk it.''

Grasping the reins in their hands, the frightened settlers pulled their horses farther into the trees until they were almost at the water's edge. Then they crouched there tensely, listening to the rustle of the leaves and the quiet murmuring of the water.

''Now what do we do, Pa?'' Samuel's voice quavered.

''Move this way,'' Elijah whispered. ''And whatever you do, keep your horse quiet.''

When they had first dismounted, they had been able to hear the hammering of horses' hooves against the hard ground. Now, however, all was

43

quiet. They began to pray, silently, asking God to take care of them and to keep the horses quiet. They were still praying when a coyote howled plaintively, his lonely cry drifting to them on the wind. At the sound, one of the horses snorted and began to fidget uneasily. Samuel felt his body tighten. Now the Indians would be sure to find them! They prayed in desperation.

Chapter 5

At Fort Robinson

Samuel squirmed about until he could watch his father, who was crouching a few yards away. The boy saw that his pa's lips were moving, and he knew that he was praying.

The three settlers knelt where they were, tensely, listening to every sound. Samuel was sure that Red was wrong about these Indians' not going into trees after their enemies. He was sure that at any instant the Indians would pounce on them, their scalping knives gleaming in the sun. He was also praying in silent desperation while the minutes stretched on with agonizing slowness, a deliberate, measured half step at a time. Still, nothing happened, and he began to relax a bit. If the Indians had heard the snort of the horse, which was by no means certain, they chose to ignore it.

He began to think that Red had known what the warriors would do after all. The wind had gone down, and a breathless hush gripped the land. An hour passed, and no sounds reached their ears but the rustling of leaves and the subdued murmuring of the water. Samuel's legs cramped, and he moved cautiously, trying to keep from making any more noise than was absolutely necessary.

The blistering sun had hung high in the heavens when the trio had dashed into the willows and hid there. Then it began to drop, silently, until it rested on the horizon.

"What're we goin' to do, Pa?" Samuel asked uneasily. They didn't have much food and water along. He wondered if the war party would be waiting for them to come out of the trees and what his pa and Red would do to try to get away from them.

"It'll be dark in a little while," Elijah answered. As soon as it was dark, they would lead their horses to the center of the shallow, twisting stream and ride east.

The boy stiffened. "Do we dare?" he asked nervously. "What if those Indians are still waitin' for us?"

"That's a chance we've got to take," Red put in. "We can't stay holed up like this. We've got a better chance of gettin' away from them in the dark than we will in the mornin'." He paused for a moment. "I think it's best to get on the move tonight."

Before leaving the safety of the willows, Elijah led his youthful companions in prayer. They bowed their heads and in soft whispers thanked God for guiding them to the trees earlier in the day and asked Him to get them safely away from the Indian war party. They all had more confidence when they had finished.

In the expectant hush of twilight Red loosed the rein of his saddle horse. Elijah and Samuel did the same. As quietly as possible, they made their way to the river bank where they waited for nightfall. It sounded to Samuel as though each crashing step through the brush was louder than a rifle shot. He prayed again that God would help the horses to be more quiet. If they weren't quiet, he reasoned, they would soon bring that war party down on them like a swarm of angry mosquitoes. And there would not be a thing he or his pa or Red could do about it.

When darkness finally came, they mounted their horses and rode east through the shallow, gurgling water. Samuel noted with relief that the normal sounds of the river effectively masked any noise their horses were making.

"How long will we stay in the water?" he asked at last.

"Another mile or so," Red told him. "That ought to be far enough to get us away from our new friends."

But they were able to stay in the stream for only a scant half mile. Then the river narrowed and got deeper. They had no choice but to leave it and go back to the prairie. Samuel had another uneasy period when they left the willows and rode out onto the prairie. He was sure the Indians were waiting for them.

But they rode all night without noticing any signs of Indians. An hour before dawn they reached the edge of the bluestem area. The grassland stretched before them, a great, undulating sea of green. Red was visibly relieved.

"Well, I don't think we're goin' to have to fret about those braves anymore," he said. "They won't be followin' us now."

"Unless they're with Standing Bear," Samuel reminded him. "He's supposed to be up here, you know."

"He's east of us quite a ways," the scout said. "And besides, Standing Bear or his men would've recognized our horses, even if they didn't recognize us. They wouldn't be givin' us any trouble."

Samuel noted the change in Red's attitude toward Standing Bear since he had received Christ. When they had left Independence, he would not have believed that any Indian could be trusted. Now he accepted the fact that Standing Bear was an honorable man and would not attack them. Elijah also caught the change in Red Terrence's attitude, but like his son, he said nothing about it.

The two boys wanted to keep on traveling that day, but when daylight was less than an hour old, the bearded settler insisted that they go into the willows and sleep for a time. They had to rest their horses, he said, and get something to eat and a little rest for themselves.

They watered their horses in the river, hobbled them and ate a cold breakfast. Even though they had managed to elude the war party, it wasn't wise for them to risk giving away their location by lighting a fire. Once they had eaten, they laid down to rest. They had only intended to sleep for an hour or so, but it was afternoon when Elijah got up and wakened his companions.

"It's time we hit the trail."

They got up, still weary from the long night of riding, ate once more and mounted their horses to continue their trip. By this time they were able to get a good picture of what the land was like. Red reined in and stood in the stirrups to look around.

"Well, Mr. Prescott," he said proudly, "what do you think of it?"

For a time the older man did not reply. The

valley stretched invitingly before them. It was entirely covered with grass, except for the wide band of willows on either side of the river. Hills reached upward from either side of the rich bottom land.

"Looks like mighty good land, Red," Elijah observed at last.

"That it is. Cows ought to do real good on grass like that."

"But that's not all," Elijah Prescott continued excitedly. "If the soil will raise that kind of grass, think what it will do with wheat and barley." An awed, almost prayerful, tone crept into his voice. "I tell you, God led us here!"

Red had to agree with him. Not only was there good soil and plenty of grass, but hundreds of cattle roamed the territory. All a person would have to do was put a rope on them. He had never thought much about settling down in one place himself, but a person could be tempted to make a place like this his home. He didn't think he would like to plow and cultivate and harvest grain, but raising cattle wouldn't be so bad. The more he thought about it, the more appealing the idea became to him.

Toward evening they reached Fort Robinson. The soldiers were surprised to see them and even more surprised to learn that they had avoided an Indian war party. Most settlers didn't know that much about Indians. Or, the commanding officer remarked, it might be that Elijah and the boys had just been lucky. He was reluctant to concede that anyone who came west to settle on a farm would know anything about Indians. The settlers he had seen were like children—they had to have someone take care of them.

Once their trail-weary horses were fed and watered, the newcomers were taken to the mess hall to eat. Colonel Grainger himself ushered them to a table. Elijah thanked him and told him he would like to have a few minutes with him the following morning.

"I'll come in and eat with you," the colonel said. "We can talk there." He paused momentarily. "How are things at Fort Laramie? Everything quiet?"

Elijah and Red told him about reaching the fort and the rash of gold fever that had broken out there. The colonel asked a few questions about it and directed the conversation to the topic of Indians. That was the thing most Army men were interested in. Were things quiet around the fort? What reports did the scouting parties bring in?

"Things are quiet around here," he said at last, "but there's no tellin' how long it's goin' to be. I've got a hunch there's somethin' cookin' among the Sioux. I don't know what it is, but I'm afraid we're all goin' to find out before too long." He pulled in a deep breath. Then, as though he had saved the most important piece of information for the last, he said, "I understand that rascal Standing Bear is comin' up into this territory again."

It disturbed Elijah to hear his friend talked about in that way, but he did not challenge Colonel Grainger.

"Are you sure about that?" Mr. Prescott asked.

The colonel picked up a pen and toyed with it thoughtfully. "There's a band of Sioux coming into these parts now," he said after a minute or two. "I haven't seen him face to face, so I can't say for sure that he's here. But I can tell you this much. There's not another chief in the whole territory who's got enough nerve to come into this area."

"They know you're here," Elijah reminded him. "Maybe seein' that nothin' has happened to you gives them the courage to come in."

Colonel Grainger squinted at him. "I don't know for sure what you're tryin' to say, but if you mean that some other chief might be around these parts, forget it. Standing Bear doesn't know what it is to be scared. There's not enough rifles and whiskey in the whole territory to get most Indians two miles off the trails around here, but that doesn't bother Standing Bear. He goes wherever he wants to." He held out his cup so an aide could pour him some more coffee. "And clever? He's the only chief I know who can disappear right in front of my men. I had a detachment out on patrol that ran into that Indian and his war party. We—"

"Are you sure it was a war party?" Elijah broke in.

The officer's temper bristled. "I know a war party when I see one. And I don't need any tenderfoot settler tellin' me what I saw. We went down in a little ravine and only lost sight of 'em for a minute. When we came up to where we could see again, they were gone. Every last one of 'em." He paused for a moment. "That Standing Bear is quite a man."

Elijah nodded. "I'd have to agree with you on that, Colonel."

Colonel Grainger's eyes narrowed. "How do you know anything about him?" he demanded.

"I met him east of Fort Kearny a month and a half ago."

The officer acted as though he didn't quite believe what the settler said. He questioned him at length about the meeting and what happened afterward.

"If you'd told me somethin' like that when I first came out here seven years ago, I would have said you were lyin' in your teeth, but I've known Standing Bear to be an honorable man. That sounds just about like what I would expect of him."

Colonel Grainger hesitated, as though he was afraid he might be leaving the wrong impression. "Now, let's get this straight. Everything I've said about that Indian is true. He's cunning. He's clever. He's honorable. But he's also ruthless and cruel. He'll do anything any of the others'll do, only he'll be quicker and more clever at it. I don't mind tellin' you that I'm more concerned about meetin' him in battle than any other chief I know of. There's not another man, white or red, who can even come close to him in strategy. He could slip in and steal your whiskers at night without even wakin' you up."

Samuel and Red both laughed.

"That might be exaggerated a little but not very much." By this time they had finished eating. The commanding officer got to his feet. "I've got to go now. If you want to talk some more, stop by my office in the mornin'."

The following day Elijah and the two boys went to see Colonel Grainger, telling him the purpose of their visit to Fort Robinson. Before they had finished, he was frowning his disapproval. He didn't approve of their wanting to settle in that area and said so. He could not keep them out if that was what they wanted to do, he told them, but they couldn't count on their supposed friendship with Standing Bear to keep them from having Indian trouble.

"Believe me," the colonel concluded, "I know!"

"I would at least like to go and talk with him," the settler said.

The officer stared at him in disbelief. "Go and talk to him?" he echoed. "What for?"

"To see if he would give us permission to settle in this area without giving us problems."

Colonel Grainger came around his desk and leaned against it. "Now I know you're out of your mind. He'll kill the lot of you before you've had a chance to tell him what you want to see him about."

When the commanding officer of the fort learned that he could not dissuade Elijah from his plan, he showed the group of settlers the place on the map where the Indians were last known to have camped.

"Just understand this," he said as Elijah and the boys were about to leave. "If you run into trouble, don't come to us for help. We've got our hands full taking care of people who've got good sense. I have no sympathy for lunatics who'll do what you're fixin' to do."

Chapter 6

Visiting Standing Bear

Elijah Prescott and the boys noted the location of Standing Bear's camp on the map once more and asked a few questions about the terrain they would be riding over. Then they left Fort Robinson. They were somewhat surprised to learn that they had to go back about 15 miles in the direction from which they had come before turning north and crossing the river. They realized they must have been fairly close to the Indian camp on their way to Fort Robinson a few days before.

With every step of their saddle horses, with every turn in the river, they prayed for guidance and safety. Elijah was quieter and more thoughtful than he had been since they had left Fort Laramie. Not only was his own life at stake, but the lives of both Samuel and Red were also in jeopardy if Colonel Grainger was correct in his appraisal of Standing Bear.

The colonel was not like some men in the west who looked on all Indians as evil and wanted to see them destroyed by any means possible. He recognized that Standing Bear was an able chief who was honorable and straightforward in all that he did. Grainger's own fairness strengthened his words.

55

Perhaps he was right about the Sioux chief's being ruthless and cruel as well.

Until that morning he had been sure Standing Bear was his friend and the friend of his family. He felt the chief appreciated what they had done for his son and would do what he could to help them. But if Grainger was correct, that would make no difference now. Standing Bear might feel that his obligation to them had been discharged.

The stocky settler had prayed long about going to the area where bluestem grass grew to see what it was like. Having looked it over, he had been sure that God was leading them to settle somewhere along the river. Even as they prayed together that morning, asking God once more to guide them and make His will known to them, he was sure they were following God's leading. Now he was troubled. What if he had made a mistake? What if God did not want them to come to this desolate area to build their home? What would happen to them then?

Samuel saw that his father was unusually quiet but did not ask him about it. He, too, was thinking about the Indian people they might be meeting. Back in the safety of the fort it had seemed exciting to think about going to an Indian camp. It was even exciting to think that they were going to a place where they might be attacked. Now, however, it was entirely different.

He wet his lips uneasily with the tip of his tongue and looked about, half expecting a war party to charge them at any instant. Again, however, he was not prepared for their sudden appearance. His father was leading them along the river, just outside the band of willows crowding along the bank, when there was a sudden stir ahead—an ominous, muffled sound. Samuel's horse shied, nostrils flaring. The movement was so sudden that he was almost thrown. Before he had time to settle himself back in the saddle, they were surrounded by warriors, arrows nocked and half drawn in their bows.

For almost a minute the hostile eyes of the braves glared at them. Samuel squirmed uncomfortably and began to wish he were back at Fort Robinson or Fort Laramie or anywhere else except where they were at that particular moment.

"Do any of you speak English?" Elijah asked at last.

The Indians gave no indication that they were aware of what he was talking about. He repeated the question slowly. By that time it was obvious that none of the Indians could understand what he was saying.

"Let Red or me try, Pa," Samuel broke in. "Lone Wolf got me started on a little sign language, and I've been workin' with Red on it ever since."

"Somebody's got to talk to them," Elijah said.

At first Samuel Prescott tried to make the braves understand that they came in peace, but he didn't succeed very well. The Indian spokesman's hands flew as he replied. Samuel had to call on Red for help.

"He is saying we do not belong here," Red explained. "He wants us to know that this is Indian country and that we are to turn around and go back."

"Ask him if Standing Bear is his chief. If he is, tell him that we are friends of the chief and would like to see him," Elijah said.

The youthful scout did as he was told.

"Their chief is Standing Bear," he said in a moment or two. "But he says we speak with a crooked tongue when we say we are friends of the chief. He says Standing Bear has no friends among the palefaces."

"See if he will take us to see Standing Bear."

The braves obviously did not want to take Elijah and the boys to their camp. After a long consultation, however, they agreed, but they insisted on taking the rifles from them first.

"I don't know whether I like this or not," Red muttered under his breath. "We're going right into that camp unarmed. We don't know for sure what's going to happen."

"It doesn't make any difference," Elijah told him. "We wouldn't use our rifles, anyway."

"I know," the boy replied, "but they don't know that."

Samuel and the others prayed silently as they were escorted to the Indian camp. They were all afraid of what might happen, but they could do nothing about it. They had to go on to the camp, unarmed, or turn around and leave the area, never to come back.

They forded the shallow river and came up over a little hill. On the opposite slope was the Indian camp, a collection of buffalo-hide tepees. A cluster of horses grazed to one side and in the center of the group of tepees was the sacred sweat lodge, an oval structure framed with willows and covered with skins. A few feet in front of the opening into the sweat lodge was the buffalo head which the warriors were expected to worship before going inside to take part in the religious ceremony.

Women were bringing firewood to their tepees or sitting cross-legged on the ground, grinding wild berries, jerky and fat with a heavy hammer. The mixture was used in making pemmican, a special food that could be stored for many months. And children were playing together in little groups, very much like they would in a white settlement.

The instant the people saw the warriors and their captives approaching, all activity in the camp ceased. Every eye turned to the warriors and the three strangers who were riding into the camp. Elijah and the boys were taken through a portion of the camp to a tepee somewhat larger than the others. There was no sign of anyone around, and Samuel would have been sure it was empty if he hadn't seen the little wisp of smoke that was spiraling up through the hole at the peak. The Indian braves did not dismount. They waited patiently astride their horses until the tepee flap opened and Standing Bear came out. He stood as straight as one of the trees along the river and carried himself regally. Lone Wolf was at his side.

Standing Bear spoke sharply to the leader of the war party in Sioux, and the man turned on his horse and said something to his companions. The white men's rifles were returned to them.

"Thank you, my friend," Elijah said to him. There was no need to use sign language with Standing Bear; he understood English.

"You are my friend," the chief told him somewhat proudly, as though it were a great honor to be considered the friend of a Sioux chief of his stature. "You took my son in and cared for him as your own. You welcomed us at your table, as though we were of your own family. Now we welcome you."

He invited Elijah and the boys to dismount. As soon as they did so, their horses were taken away. At first Samuel wondered what was happening, but then he realized that they were only taking the horses to feed and water them.

Standing Bear invited them into his tepee and had his wife serve them pemmican and some little cakes made of ground corn. For an hour or more after they had finished eating, the chief talked with Elijah and the boys. He wanted to know about Mrs. Prescott and Becky. He was particularly interested in Becky and called for his own daughter, who was about her age, so Elijah could meet her. He wanted to know what had happened on the trail since he last saw them. After a time the conversation lapsed into a long silence. Elijah sensed that he should state the purpose of their journey.

He began by telling Standing Bear about the lack of scouts and their concern about not being able to make the trip all the way across the mountain ranges before winter. So he and the boys had come to the area to look over the land. They wanted to see whether it was the sort of place they wanted to settle in.

For an instant Standing Bear's face grew hard. "And why come to me?" he demanded harshly.

"When the chief at Fort Robinson said you were in this area, I decided to come and talk to you," Elijah told him, referring to Colonel Grainger. "I wanted to see if you would object to our being here."

The chief had some questions to ask. Why did

they choose that particular area? Did they plan to stay only for the winter? Or would they be moving on in the spring? Would they try to kill off the buffalo as was being done elsewhere on the Great Plains? Elijah answered him as truthfully as possible. When Standing Bear had heard Elijah's answers, he arose abruptly.

"Wait!" he said, gesturing quickly. "This is a matter for the council." He went outside, talked briefly with one of the braves and returned.

"We will discuss this matter when the council comes here at the setting of the sun."

There was nothing for the settlers to do but wait. They roamed at will around the camp, watching the children play and the women at work scraping hides, making moccasins or drying meat for the winter. Not until the council gathered in Standing Bear's tepee at sundown would Elijah be allowed to continue.

Most of those on the tribal council were older men, but this did not surprise Elijah and his companions. The Indians greatly respected age and gave positions of trust and high honor to those who had lived for a long while.

Each man conducted himself with great dignity. These were men of authority, and their bearing revealed it. They greeted the newcomers gravely before sitting across from them.

"I will repeat in Sioux what you say," Standing Bear explained, "so they can all understand." He then asked Elijah to explain the purpose for his visit.

The bearded settler repeated his request, giving his reason for wanting to settle in that area. They all listened intently, even though they could not understand. Standing Bear repeated in Sioux everything that Elijah said. Now and then a council member broke in with a question. They wanted to know how many people would be coming with Elijah, where they would settle and if they had plans to bring in others later. Mr. Prescott was careful to answer each question honestly.

Only his family would be coming, he said. They had not yet chosen a place, but they would likely settle fairly close to the river and within a few miles of Fort Robinson. He could not say that others would not come. This he had no way of knowing, but he would do nothing himself to bring more settlers. After a long while Standing Bear dismissed him.

"We will discuss the matter tonight," he said. "Tomorrow we will give you our answer. Tomorrow, while the sun is still climbing the mountain in the sky."

The councilmen stirred, which was a signal to Elijah that the time had come for the trio to leave. He thanked Standing Bear and the others for their time and took Samuel and Red outside.

Once they were outside Standing Bear's tepee, Samuel turned to his father. "What do you think, Pa?" he asked softly. "Do you think they're going to let us settle here?"

"It's in God's hands now," Elijah answered. "If He wants us to live here, He'll work in their hearts and make them willing to have us."

When Samuel went to sleep that night, he did so to the sound of his father's voice. He was asking God to work in the deliberations of the council so His will for them would be done.

Chapter 7

Building a Home

Shortly after sunrise the following morning one of the women brought a breakfast of dried berries and pemmican to the tepee the white men had been allowed to use overnight. When the men had finished eating, Standing Bear appeared with two of his councilmen—sturdy, hardfaced warriors who looked as though they never smiled. Samuel wondered why there were there. The chief did not introduce them and neither spoke a word.

"We discussed your request all night," Standing Bear began in his calm, deliberate manner. "Some of our young men do not like it that you came to us. They hate all white men and wanted to kill you."

Elijah Prescott did not look or act upset, but Red and Samuel shuddered. They both knew that Standing Bear and his men were quite capable of doing anything.

But the Indian leader drew himself erect. "But in honor, we could not do that," he continued. "You came in peace; you shall go in peace."

The 13-year-old Prescott boy relaxed slightly. A prayer of thanksgiving moved his lips in silence. Yet his heart was heavy. He knew the chief's answer now. They were not going to get permission to settle in the area. What would they do? What *could* they do?

However, Standing Bear had not finished talking.

"The white man comes like swarms of grasshoppers," he said. "They are so many they darken the sun. Soon there will be so many, there will be no room left for the buffalo—no room for the Indian. We will be driven from the land of our fathers."

He paused, hatred and fear gleaming in his eyes. "But our council has decided that keeping you out or letting you stay among us will not change the flood of white men. Your words are as straight as a hunting arrow. You have shown us that you are our friend. Coming here to ask our permission shows that you have respect for us and our rights."

Standing Bear's expression changed. "So we have decided that it is good for us to have your kind among us. You will never have anything to fear from me or from my people. As long as you remain our friend, we will walk in peace together."

Waves of joy swept over Samuel. He glanced at Red, grinning his relief. They all silently thanked God for working through Standing Bear and his council.

*　　*　　*

On the way back to Fort Laramie they saw a settler's house in the distance and rode over to introduce themselves. A young couple by the name of Borman had moved there earlier in the spring and built the house.

"My friends call me Tex," the young man said, thrusting out his hand impulsively. "I rode trail up this way for two or three years and saw a lot of stray longhorns just waitin' for somebody to drop a rope on 'em. So when Nellie and I decided to get married, we came up here and built a house. We're fixin' to run cattle. And we'll make it, too, if those cursed Indians will only leave us alone."

Samuel wanted to protest that Tex shouldn't have such an attitude toward the Indians, but his pa had taught him to respect those who were older than himself. Even though he didn't like what the young rancher said, he remained silent.

Elijah and the boys were going to go on, but Tex and Nellie Borman insisted that they join them for dinner. Mrs. Borman was particularly anxious to have them stay for a little while.

"You're the only white people we've seen since we got here, except for Hans and Greta Maier and the Crowell brothers. They've got places up the river a little ways," she said. "Come in and sit so you can tell me about your wife while I fix dinner. You don't know how hungry for new faces a person can get in a place as lonesome as this."

They went into the one-room sod house and sat on the packing cases the Bormans used for chairs while she fixed something to eat. Elijah told her about Hannah and Becky. She had a hundred questions about them and was anxious to have them move close by.

"Greta Maier is a lovely person," she explained, "but she doesn't speak English, and I don't know any German. And the Crowell boys aren't even married. It'll be so good to have another woman close by so I can have someone to talk to once in a while."

Tex was as anxious as his wife to have another family in the area but for a different reason. "We need all the whites we can get," he said. "Havin' you out here'll mean two or three more rifles in case Standing Bear goes on the rampage again."

Elijah did not like the tone of his voice as he spoke about the Indian chief. "I find Standing Bear quite agreeable," he said mildly.

Tex growled at him. "I get all-fired tired of you sodbusters from the East who come out here just burstin' with brotherly love and kindness toward those savages. When you get to know 'em, you'll know how wrong you are. I tell you, Prescott, you can't trust any of 'em! And that goes double for Standing Bear!"

Mrs. Borman was pouring more coffee, and Elijah held out his cup to have it filled. "We probably haven't been out here as much as you have, but we have had quite a little to do with the Indians since we left home back East. I've found that if you treat the Indians with the courtesy and respect a Christian ought to show other people, they'll treat you the same way."

Tex swore angrily. "I'm goin' to tell you what to do. You write down what you said just now. Write it plain, and put it in a place where you can get your hands on it in a year. Make that six months. After you've lived among 'em for that long, you'll find out how much you can trust those savages." He swore again. "If I had my way, I'd turn the Army loose on 'em and not call 'em back 'till we'd driven every last Indian so high into the mountains they couldn't ever find their way back."

Elijah tried to change the subject, but Borman wasn't quite ready to give up and continued to mouth his hatred and fear of the Sioux. Samuel's pa refused to argue with him. He stated his position and changed the subject. Samuel was still thinking about it when they had finished eating and finally left the Bormans.

"I don't know whether I'd want to be friends with him or not," Samuel said. "I didn't like what he had to say about Standing Bear."

"Neither did I," Elijah answered. "But I think he hates the chief because he doesn't really know him. And he's really afraid of him. If he knew Standing Bear the way we do, he would like him and respect him."

Samuel's eyes flashed. "He's never goin' to change his mind about them. He made me so mad I—I don't even know whether I want to be neighbors to them or not."

"We shouldn't feel that way," Elijah continued thoughtfully. "We just need to pray for Tex Borman and the others like him so God will take away the hatred in their hearts."

*　　　*　　　*

The trip back to Fort Laramie on horseback and the return to the Fort Robinson area with their wagon and oxen took almost two weeks. The Prescotts and Red Terrence were eagerly looking forward to settling down in one place.

"It seems to me that we've been travelin' in this wagon for ever and ever," Becky said to her mother the last afternoon of their trip. "We won't know what it's like to stay in one place."

"We probably won't have enough time to think about what it will be like," Mrs. Prescott answered. "We're goin' to have to cut sod and build a house first. Then we've got to build some kind of a shelter for the horses and oxen and get some grass cut." She hesitated, almost overwhelmed by all the work they had to do before winter. "We've got to be prayin' that God will give us time and strength to get everything done before cold weather."

Becky was only half aware of the reason for her mother's concern. At the moment the afternoon was so warm and pleasant, she could not imagine that they would have a lot of work to do before winter. At least there seemed to be plenty of time. She sighed luxuriously. "Just the same, I'm goin' to be so glad we won't have to keep travelin' all the time."

*   *   *

" 'Dear Diary,

" 'Pa rode on ahead yesterday to check again on the place where we're goin' to build our house. He came back after dark last night, all excited about the place he found. It's about a mile from Tex Borman's. It's right down in the valley, not far from the river, and there are the most beautiful hills all around us. At least that's what Pa says. We can hardly wait to see it.' "

Trena stopped reading momentarily and looked up at Grandma Redding, who was sitting in the easy chair next to her.

68

"Is that this place, Grandma? Where we live now?" she asked.

The gray-haired woman nodded. "I reckon so. Of course, Elijah Prescott didn't build the house you live in. The first house on the place was built of sod, but it stood not far from where this home is now. It was still standing when I was a little girl."

Trena studied her lined face wistfully. She wished she had lived back then or at the time Becky Prescott had been a little girl. That would have been exciting!

*   *   *

The Prescotts continued to live in their wagon until they had cut sod and piled up the heavy blocks to build a crude sod house. The wagon provided enough boards to build doors and windows. The sod house they put up was not very large, and it certainly was not as nice as the house they had lived in back East. But when they had finally finished working on it, they thought it was the grandest house in all the world.

That night they had a time of special thanksgiving. They thanked God for guiding them to the place near the river and for giving them good weather so they were able to get their house finished. They thanked Him, too, for giving Standing Bear and his people warm hearts toward them so they were willing to let them settle in the area. They were still praying when Tex Borman rode up. The entire family went to the door to meet him.

"Howdy, Tex," Elijah said. "Won't you come in and have some supper?"

Borman squinted at the setting sun. "I don't reckon I ought to take time for eating right now. I've got to go over and see the Crowells and give 'em the news."

Hannah Prescott caught the concern in his voice. "Is there something wrong?" she asked.

"There's somethin' wrong, all right. There's a big herd of buffalo in these parts. Nellie and I saw the dust this mornin' and went to take a look. I tell you, there're more buffalo in that herd than I've seen in one place for the past ten years."

"I'm glad to know that," Elijah said. "Red and I'll have to see what we can do about gettin' a couple for meat."

The newcomer shook his head incredulously. "You still don't know much about what's goin' on, do you, Prescott? I came here to warn you. Wherever there's buffalo, there's Indians! And where there's Indians, there's trouble. And don't you forget it."

He acted as though he was about to whirl and go galloping away, but he turned back for a last warning. "Keep your eyes peeled, Prescott. Those Indians will be after buffalo, but they'll be on the lookout for anything else they can lay their thievin' hands on! So don't leave this place of yours alone—even for a few minutes! If you do, you're a bigger fool than I think you are!"

Chapter 8

Indian Visitors

When Tex Borman finally disappeared over the hill to the south, Elijah turned thoughtfully and went back into the house. He tried to keep from showing his concern but did not succeed very well. It showed through in spite of himself.

Becky held out her hand for the strength and warmth of his big, rough fingers. She was a little bit afraid after hearing Tex Borman and wanted reassurance from her pa. "You don't think those Indians will hurt us, do you?" she asked.

"Of course not," he answered. "We don't have to worry about Standing Bear's band. He gave us his word that we would be safe, and I trust him."

Her smile flashed at him. "I'm glad we made friends with Standing Bear and Lone Wolf, aren't you?"

*   *   *

When the boys were helping Elijah work on a barn for their cattle and oxen, Red asked the older man the same question Trena had put into words. He gave the same answer.

"But what if some other Indians come into this

area followin' the herd?" the boy asked. "What if a band shows up that hasn't heard of the arrangement we made with the chief?"

Elijah stopped working momentarily. "I've been thinkin' about that too."

"That isn't what we were told back at Fort Laramie," Samuel put in. "Don't you remember, Pa? The guys who'd been up here said the Indians were scared to come into this area. Standing Bear and his band were the only ones who weren't afraid."

"That's what we were told, all right," his father replied. "But how long do you think it's goin' to stay that way? When the other Indians see that Standing Bear and his people are livin' here without any trouble and that we came in, along with the Army and ranchers like Tex Borman, it won't be long 'til they get the idea it's as safe here as it is anywhere else."

Red agreed with Elijah. "I've been tryin' to make myself believe the other Indians are scared to come in here, but I know I'm just kiddin' myself. I reckon there's a good chance of a war party comin' our way any time."

Elijah laid a hand on the young scout's shoulder. "Let's not say anything to Hannah and Becky about this. OK? At least till we know for sure there's goin' to be trouble."

Shortly after sunrise the following morning Tex Borman rode into the yard. At first the Prescotts thought he had brought more news of the buffalo and the Indians he was sure would be following the herd. But that wasn't the purpose of his visit. He called Elijah to one side and talked

72

with him in low tones for several minutes. Samuel and Becky watched uneasily.

"What do you suppose that's all about?" she asked.

He shrugged. "How would I know?"

"Maybe he's found out something bad about Standing Bear, and he came over to tell Pa."

But Samuel didn't think so. If that was what had brought Tex Borman to their place, he'd have blurted it out for them all to hear. That's what he had done before. He wouldn't care if the whole world knew something bad about Standing Bear. The more Samuel considered the matter, the more sure he was that Tex Borman had something else on his mind.

Finally, Tex finished talking and started toward the hitching rail where he had tied his horse. Elijah walked with him. His hand on the reins, Tex turned back. "You don't know how much I appreciate this."

"Think nothin' of it. Hannah'll be glad to go over and talk to her."

Tex's voice grew louder until Samuel and Becky could hear everything he said without difficulty. "It'd be better if Hannah could go this mornin'," he continued. "I've never seen Nellie go to pieces like this. She's got her mind set on packin' up everything we own and headin' back to Texas first thing in the mornin'."

Elijah studied his visitor's lean young face. "Are you fixin' to go?" he asked.

"Not if I can help it," he said nervously. "But I can't let her go traipsin' off all by herself. And that's what she says she's goin' to do if I won't go along. I tell you, she's not herself these days. Since

73

she found out about that herd and the possibility of Indians followin' it, she's gettin' too scared to go out of the house."

When Tex rode off a moment later, Elijah went inside and told his wife the purpose of Tex's visit. "I told him you'd go over and try to talk some sense into her."

Mentally Hannah went over what she had to do that morning. She was making bread, for one thing. She would have to finish that before she left. And she had planned to wash clothes. Of course, the washing could be put off for another day or two.

"I'll go as soon as I finish baking bread, Elijah," she told him.

"Can't Becky take care of that?"

"I'd like to go along, Pa," Becky broke in.

"I don't reckon that'd be best this time," he told her. "Nellie Borman might want to talk to Ma alone."

Hannah couldn't leave her daughter with all of the bread making. She would have to finish kneading the dough herself, forming it into loaves and putting it into the pans. Becky would know when the loaves were ready to bake—she had helped often enough.

"I'll be ready in an hour," she told her husband.

"Want me to take Ma over to the Bormans?" Samuel asked, hoping his pa didn't realize how curious he was to find out why Mrs. Borman wanted to leave so suddenly. "I could hitch the oxen to the wagon."

"To go a mile?" his father laughed. "Ma can walk or ride your saddle horse. We're goin' to start on a firebreak around the buildings. It's gettin' so

74

dry that I'm concerned about it. A flash of lightnin' and we'd have ourselves a fire like you've never seen before."

Samuel yoked the oxen to the plow and began to circle the buildings, turning over the dry sod. He had never even heard of a firebreak until they stopped at Tex Borman's the first time. The rancher had plowed a wide strip around his buildings to stop any grass fire that might come their way. Red had told Samuel what it was for. He hadn't even thought of it again until his father told him to plow a firebreak around their house and barn.

Hannah Prescott rode her son's saddle horse to the Borman house. When she got there, Nellie was sitting at the kitchen table, her eyes red and swollen. She looked up as Hannah approached the door.

"It's not goin' to do you any good," she muttered.

"I just came to talk to you," Mrs. Prescott said.

"I've got my mind made up," Nellie retorted defensively. "I'm leavin' here for home. And if Tex wants to come along, he's welcome. But I can't stand it any more. I—" She started to cry again.

Lovingly, Hannah sat down beside her and wrapped her arms about her. At first she let her cry without saying very much. That seemed to quiet the upset woman. When she relaxed a little, Mrs. Prescott began to talk with her. She did not try to laugh away Nellie's fears or make her believe that the danger was all in her mind. She admitted, quite frankly, that she was afraid herself.

"Do you know what I do when I'm afraid?" she asked her young friend. "I tell God about it

75

and ask Him to give me the strength to overcome my fears." She went on talking, telling Nellie how Jesus Christ had removed her worries and had given her happiness and contentment to replace her agony.

Mrs. Borman didn't know anything about being a Christian. She had gone to Sunday school a few times when she was a child, but she couldn't remember hearing anything about sin or about trusting Christ.

*　　*　　*

It was late in the afternoon when Hannah Prescott rode across the new firebreak and dismounted. Samuel came running from the barn to take the horse.

"I'll water him for you, Ma," he said.

She smiled gratefully.

"What about Mrs. Borman?" he asked. By this time the others knew Mrs. Prescott was home. Becky came out of the house, and Elijah and Red walked in their direction from across the opposite firebreak. "Did you talk her into staying?"

"To tell you the truth, Samuel," she replied, "I didn't even try."

He was surprised and told her so. He thought that was the purpose of the visit.

"No," she went on, "we were too busy talking about other things. Her real need was Jesus Christ. She's a Christian now, and you never saw such a change in a person. I don't think there'll be any more talk about her wanting to leave to go back home."

"That's wonderful!" Elijah said. He followed

76

his wife into their little sod house and dropped heavily to a chair. "Now we'll have to pray twice as hard for Tex."

The rancher later told them he was grateful for the change in his wife, even though he was bewildered by it.

"I don't understand all this talk about God," he said, "but it doesn't matter. It changed Nellie in a way you wouldn't believe. I'm happy for it."

*　　*　　*

Elijah Prescott's birthday was approaching, and an air of expectancy and mystery encompassed the little sod house. There were many whispered conferences between Becky and her mother. There were knowing smiles, and there was feverish activity. Becky seemed to be the one in charge of arrangements. At least she was the one who made Samuel and Red promise not to tell what she and her mother was planning.

There was to be a surprise party for their pa the next night. She wanted them to slip over to the Borman place and ask Tex and Nellie to come for supper. But they were to be warned not to say a word to their pa about it.

"We want to surprise him," she explained.

"You'll have a hard time doin' that," Red told her. "Look at everything that's goin' on around here. He'd have to be blind not to know somethin's up."

For an instant Becky was hurt. Then her eyes brightened. Come to think of it, she didn't believe her pa even remembered it was his birthday. "And

77

if we're all careful not to give it away, he won't remember either."

Elijah Prescott had planned to break some more sod that morning, but at breakfast he decided to put off the plowing and check the buffalo herd. He asked Red to go with him.

"We'll take our rifles along," he said. "If they're still around, which I doubt, we'll see if we can get some meat."

Samuel wanted to go along, but his father wanted him to hitch up the wagon and drive the oxen down to the river to fill the barrels with water. That was a job Samuel especially disliked, but he did not argue about it. Everyone in the family had to do a lot of things they didn't particularly like.

He had finished his task and was in the barn taking the yoke off the oxen when he heard the pounding of horses' hooves. He went to the barn door and looked out. At first he thought it must be his pa and Red. Then he saw three Indian riders galloping their mounts down the trail straight for the sod house!

Samuel's first impulse was to whirl and run, but there was no time for that. They were already across the firebreak and into the yard. They jerked their mounts to a halt and leaped effortlessly to the ground. Then they trooped to the door, opened it and stomped inside!

Fear gripped the boy, making it hard for him to breathe.

Chapter 9

Fire!

Sweat stood out on Samuel's forehead and his body was trembling violently. Those Indians had gone straight into the house. And his ma and Becky were there alone! All the terrible things he had ever heard about Indian braves and what they did to their captives flashed through his mind. Nausea sent pains into his stomach and almost put him on his knees.

His first thought was of the rifle. He wished his pa had left it in the barn or with him. Almost as quickly as the thought came, he realized how foolish it was. What would he do with the rifle if he had it? Would he shoot one of the Indian men? Would he shoot all three of them? He didn't even know why they had come or what they were doing.

He could get his saddle horse and ride over to Tex Borman's for help, but that wouldn't be wise, he knew. The Bormans lived a mile away. By the time he got back, the braves would have had time to take his mother and sister back to their camp with them. Even if they hadn't left by the time he got back, the rancher from Texas could not be trusted. He had already decided that the only

Indian who could be trusted was a dead Indian. Tex would just make matters worse.

Carefully, Samuel crept toward the window and peered into the house. The buckskin-clad strangers stood inside the door, looking about curiously. Now that he was able to get a good look at the men, he saw that one of them, the leader of the trio, had been at Standing Bear's side the morning the chief told his pa that they could settle in the valley. He was one of the ruling council. Samuel relaxed slightly. Perhaps he wasn't so dangerous after all.

"Me Gray Thunder," the spokesman said in broken English. "We hungry."

So that was it! They had come to the house to get food. Samuel had heard his pa talk about the Indians and their customs. He mentioned that it was customary to go to the tepee of someone else in the tribe if they were hungry. And their culture demanded that the guests be fed.

In desperation Samuel prayed that he was right—that the Indian men had only come for something to eat.

His mother was frightened—he saw that in her eyes. But she was as kind and hospitable as ever. "Won't you sit down?" she asked, motioning to the chairs. "I'll fix something for you right away."

At first they did not understand her, and she repeated her invitation. Although she gestured toward the chairs, they grunted something Samuel could not hear and sat down on the floor, watching Mrs. Prescott and Becky with great interest.

Becky's hands were trembling so much as she rolled out the cookies she was making that Samuel wondered if she would be able to continue. But she did, using a cutter her pa had made for her a long while ago. She was so nervous she might have let the first batch burn if her mother had not reminded her that they were ready.

"Oh, I almost forgot them!" she cried. She set the flat cookie sheet on the table. The cookies were a delicate golden brown, and the aroma filled the little sod house.

Samuel straightened cautiously to see what else was going on in the little house. As he did so, Gray Thunder's gaze met his. He ducked involuntarily, as though hoping to avoid being seen. He grinned sheepishly. Why should he stay outside? Now they knew he was around.

When he opened the door, his ma handed him a bucket and asked him to fill it with fresh water. "We have company, Samuel," she said. "I want to make tea for them."

In a moment he was back, setting the water on a small stand just inside the door.

Gray Thunder and his companions paid little attention to Samuel, however; they were staring at Becky.

"We hungry," the spokesman repeated, as though there had been some great breach of good manners by postponing the matter so long. "We hungry. We eat." He pointed to the cookies.

"They are too hot yet," Becky told him hurriedly. "You'll have to wait until they cool!"

Samuel saw the questions in the Indian mens' eyes and realized that Becky had talked so fast they had not understood her. He was quite sure they were comparing this experience to one in an Indian friend's home where they probably would not have had to wait half so long.

"Too hot," Samuel explained slowly. He enunciated his words with care. "They are as hot as a thousand fires. Wait until the flames go out of them. Then eat!"

He picked up one of the cookie sheets with a towel and took it over to Gray Thunder so the Indian spokesman could feel the heat that would have burned their mouths. Gray Thunder said something in Sioux and settled back against the wall. His companions did the same.

By the time Becky had baked another pan of cookies, the first batch was cool enough to eat. Samuel gave cookies to each of them. Gray Thunder bit into his hesitantly, as though fearing the taste. Then his face brightened.

"Good!" he exclaimed. "Much good!" He gobbled up his cookie and held out his hand for more.

"Samuel!" Becky exclaimed in a hoarse whisper. "Don't let them have all of them! I'm baking these cookies for Pa's birthday party."

"We've got to give them a few more," he said, speaking rapidly and keeping his voice low enough so their guests would not understand. "These men have come to us for food the way they would go to a tepee in their band. If we are going to make friends with them, we have to feed them."

"But we're having company for supper and everything!" she protested. Tears came to her eyes, and for an instant Samuel was sure his sister was going to cry.

At that moment Elijah and Red came riding up. The little group in the sod house didn't hear them until they flung the door open and charged in, not knowing what they would find.

"We hungry," Gray Thunder was repeating. He held out his hand to the 11-year-old girl. Reluctantly, she gave him another. By this time, Hannah had something else ready for their Indian guests to eat. Elijah and Red sat down with them, sharing the food.

Gray Thunder spoke English haltingly, but well enough to make himself understood. His companions, however, knew only three or four words in the strange tongue. After several attempts to talk to them, Red and Samuel switched to sign language. They asked where the trio had been hunting and if they had done well. The men were from Standing Bear's band. There was no doubt of that now, although Samuel had been sure from the first. They had killed some buffalo, and the women were drying the meat and tanning the hides. But they still had to have much more food and many buffalo hides for the winter.

When the Indians had finally finished eating and had asked for more cookies, they got to their feet to leave. By this time Gray Thunder had also switched to sign language. He began to talk to the boys hurriedly with his hands, and they both laughed.

"What did he say?" Becky wanted to know. She could tell by the way the Indian men looked at her that Gray Thunder had said something about her.

"He wants us to ask Pa if he'll sell you," Samuel said, laughing. "He'd like to take you back to his family. He said all you would have to do would be to make those 'little breads' for them."

She flushed scarlet. "I—I—" she sputtered.

Gray Thunder laughed. Only then did she realize that he was teasing her.

When the Indians were gone, Samuel came back into the sod house, grinning broadly. "Know something, Becky?" he asked. "I think maybe Gray Thunder had a good idea. We'll sell you to him."

She snorted her indignation. "Just for that you don't get any cookies tonight!"

Elijah looked puzzled. "Is something special happening tonight?" he asked. "Why do we need cookies anyway?"

"Well, Pa, I . . . I mean, we . . ." stammered Becky.

Mrs. Prescott broke in. "Now, don't be asking so many questions, Elijah. You'll see why we need cookies later."

Becky was sure her pa had guessed that they were planning his birthday party. But when the Bormans arrived at suppertime and wished him a happy birthday, he was really surprised.

"Why, I'd completely forgotten it," he laughed. As they all sat down at the table, he turned to Becky. "So that's why you baked all those cookies. I couldn't figure that out at all!"

*   *   *

The blazing heat of late August had sucked the last trace of green from the grass. Hannah Prescott's little garden had long since dried up, and the soil was as empty of moisture as gunpowder. And the sky gave no hope that the rains would come soon. Day after day it remained cloudless, except for an occasional dark cloud, hanging over

84

the horizon. And occasionally lightning leaped from one distant black mass to another.

Elijah Prescott tried to ignore the ominous heat as he and the boys worked to get ready for winter. They were busy from dawn until the last trace of twilight had disappeared and the valley had fallen into silence and shadows. Then the smell of smoke drifted in on the parched wind, and the western sky took on a threatening hue.

"Looks as though that fire we've been concerned about has finally come," he said, fighting against the sickening fear in his heart.

"It won't get to us, will it, Pa?" Becky asked fearfully.

He told her he didn't think it would, but they began to pray even more earnestly about the fire, asking God to spare them. The next morning Elijah sent Samuel and Red out with the oxen to plow more furrows around their buildings.

At first it seemed that God was answering their prayers. The smoke that hung over the western horizon seemed to be fading away. Every afternoon black, rolling thunderheads tumbled over the horizon and clawed their way up the steep canopy of sky. Becky began to relax. She knew the worst of the fires must be over.

Elijah said little about it, but he was beginning to agree with her. He was sure it would rain soon. He was also thinking about getting some more meat for winter. He and Red had killed one buffalo the last time they had gone out, and the whole family had pitched in to help Hannah prepare the meat. Another animal would be that much more insurance against running out before spring. This time he agreed that Samuel could join him and Red Terrence.

They set out at dawn the following morning, ignoring the clouds that hung low in the west. Mrs. Prescott and Becky watched the rolling thunderheads as they moved closer and closer. Lightning stabbed from one cloud to another, and the thunder rolled.

"I sure hope we get some rain, don't you?" Becky asked.

"That's what we've been praying for," her mother reminded her. "Maybe God is going to answer us now."

And then they saw the smoke roll upward from the other side of the hill. It was dark and hot, spiraling up toward the sun. There was no doubt about it—the smoke was billowing higher than ever. They could even see the angry red tips of the flames that were fanned high by the rising wind.

"Fire! And it's coming right for us!" Becky cried. "What are we goin' to do?"

Hannah was staring at the sod house. The dark squares of earth were covered with grass, sucked as dry as tinder by the sun. A spark would be enough to set the grass in the sod aflame like so much coal oil.

"Quick, Becky!" she shouted. "We've got to get buckets and wet down the house and barn!"

They worked frantically, filling the buckets from the big barrels of water Samuel brought from the river and throwing it on the sod house and barn. The sod drank the water thirstily.

Becky was glad for something to do. Each effort was a prayer for help. Just knowing that they were making some small contribution in the fight against the terrible flames gave her strength and courage. At last the task was finished. The house and barn were thoroughly soaked, and the last of the water was gone. Exhausted, they sank to the ground.

Chapter 10

Lost Cattle

Becky and her mother were still in the yard, trembling with emotion and staring at the smoke as it drew closer. They had not moved when Nellie Borman came riding up on one of her husband's saddle horses. They were so caught up in the spectacle that was approaching them that they didn't even hear the hard-running horse until he hammered across the rock-hard prairie near their house and was jerked to a halt not three feet from them.

The Borman horse's chest was heaving, and his nostrils were flared. Nellie slipped from the back of the hard-breathing animal and would have collapsed at Hannah Prescott's feet if the older woman had not grabbed her and held her up.

"Nellie!" Becky's ma cried. "Are you all right?" Her face was stark and rigid, frozen with terror. She tried to speak, but the words would not come. Hannah repeated her question.

"I—I think I'm all right," Mrs. Borman managed. Then she tried to explain why she had come to the Prescott home. "Tex is away, and I—I just had to come over here when I saw the fire was h-heading our way. I couldn't stand it at home alone for another minute." Her eyes pleaded with the other woman not to send her away.

"Everything's goin' to be all right," Hannah assured her. "Don't you fret, Nellie."

"Are—are you sure?" the younger woman asked doubtfully.

Hannah hesitated a moment before going on. "God tells us in the Bible that all things work together for good to those who love God," she said. "Since we know that's true, everything that happens to us is goin' to be a help for us. God makes it come out that way."

Nellie thought about that. It hardly seemed possible to her that what her friend said could be true, but watching Hannah and Becky made her more sure that it was. It wasn't natural for anyone to be as calm and unruffled as the girl and her ma were. The only explanation that made sense was that their peace came from God.

As the fire swept toward the sod house and barn, the two women and Becky knelt and asked God to spare them, if it was His will. One or two sparks flew across the firebreak and landed on the roof of the house, but it was so damp from the water they had thrown on it that it did not catch fire. Another spark landed a few feet from where Hannah, Becky and Nellie were praying. But Hannah stomped it out before it burned more than a handful of grass.

Then the flames raced on either side of the firebreak, joined again on the other side and rushed on, leaving an island of brown, dry grass surrounded by the charred prairie bluestem.

"Thank God the fire is gone!" Nellie breathed prayerfully.

After a time of thanksgiving and prayer, Hannah offered to go back to the Borman place with Nellie, to be with her in case the fire had not spared her home. Her friend assured her that she needed no one with her, however.

"I have to learn to trust God the way you do," she murmured. "I—I believe I learned something today about the way He takes care of us."

"It doesn't always mean that everything turns out for us the way we want it to," Hannah reminded her. She didn't go on, but she was thinking about the Borman buildings. It just might be that God had allowed Tex and Nellie's home and barn to be damaged by the prairie fire in order to help them spiritually.

Nellie was thinking about that too. "I believe I could handle things now, even if I did get home and find our place burned," she said. "It might be that God wanted to teach us how to learn to depend on Him."

However, the buildings of the other settlers were also left untouched. The Prescotts thanked God for that.

The grass in the area was destroyed. That in itself wasn't a serious problem. It just meant that they would have to let their cattle and oxen graze farther from the buildings in order to find forage. And it wasn't going to be so easy for them to get hay to keep their livestock through the winter.

"But we can make it," Elijah said confidently. "With God's help we can put up enough hay and get it hauled over here to have the feed we need 'til spring."

Samuel was grateful for his pa. He was one man who never took credit for things himself. He always acknowledged that God was helping him. And he didn't have any trouble praying for guidance, either, or letting people know that he sought the will of God for his life. If they didn't like it, that was their problem.

Elijah and Red helped Samuel catch the lead cow. The boys held her so Mr. Prescott could put a larger bell around her neck. "Now," he said, signaling for the boys to let her go, "we ought to be able to locate you a little easier, Old Girl."

"Where're we goin' to take our cattle and oxen to graze?" Samuel wanted to know.

"There's only one way we can go," Red put in, "and that's toward the river. They've got to have some water."

Elijah agreed with him—not that the cattle could be kept from the water. It always seemed to him that cattle could smell water a lot farther than anyone gave them credit for. Even if the cattle were driven into the hills in the opposite direction from the river, they would probably head for the river, unless they happened to find a closer source of water.

*   *   *

Several days later Tex Borman and Amos Crowell came over to find out if the Prescotts were missing any cattle. Both of them had experienced sizeable losses. Crowell lost his oxen as well as his cattle, and Tex could find only his horses. The rest of his livestock were gone.

"We thought we'd come over and see how things were with you," Tex stated irritably. It was obvious that he had already made up his mind about what had happened.

"I sent Samuel out to check 'em this afternoon," Elijah said. "He ought to be back any time."

"Unless you're a lot luckier than the rest of us," Tex said grumpily, "you'll have the same problem we've got! And we know what's happened. It's them cursed savages! We're goin' to have to get the Army to roust 'em out of here and keep 'em out, or we're done for."

"We shouldn't be so quick to blame the Indians for it. The cattle could have strayed. That happens, you know."

Tex palmed the saddle horn with his left hand and leaned forward, anger and hatred mingling in his narrowing eyes. "My cattle could stray, maybe. Or Crowell's, or yours. I could buy that. But all of 'em at once? Don't make me laugh, Prescott. Those cattle didn't stray! They just provided old Standing Bear with some easy meat. Go into his camp right now, and you'll find plenty of red and white hides!"

"I don't even know that anything has happened to mine," the settler reminded him.

Tex was looking past him at Samuel, who was riding toward the buildings at a fast trot. "Here comes Samuel without any cattle. Ask him whether he could find 'em or not."

"I told him to check on 'em, not bring 'em in."

But when his son got close enough so he could see his face, he knew that they, too, had lost their livestock.

"I looked and looked and looked, Pa," Samuel said, "but I couldn't find any of them. There wasn't any sign of 'em anywhere."

"What'd I tell ya?" Tex demanded triumphantly. "Now're you goin' to try to argue that the Indians didn't have anything to do with this?"

"We certainly don't know that they did," Elijah reminded him.

Tex swore. "What do you have to have? A sign a hundred feet high sayin' 'We did it!' " He leaned forward once more. "We're goin' to have a meetin' over at our house tonight, Elijah! We're goin' to figure out what we've got to do to keep the savages from gettin' our cattle! You'd better be there!"

Before Mr. Prescott had an opportunity to reply, Tex and Amos rode off at a brisk gallop.

Elijah wasn't sure at first that he was going to the meeting. He didn't want to show up, because it might make them believe he was condoning any decision they might make. After praying about it, however, he decided to go.

"Maybe I can hammer some sense into Tex and the Crowells," he said.

"We'll be prayin' for you, Elijah," Hannah told him quietly.

He laid a rough hand on her arm, nodding his gratitude. "I'm sure goin' to need it," he told her quietly.

It was late when he got back from the meeting with the neighbors, but everyone was still up.

"Would they listen to you, Pa?" Samuel asked.

Mr. Prescott shook his head. "They never heard a word I said." He was so dejected that his voice was empty and lifeless. "I might as well have stayed home."

94

"But you tried, Pa," Becky said loyally. "You did the best you could."

"It wasn't good enough, I'm afraid," he replied miserably. "There's goin' to be trouble between the settlers and the Indians—plenty of it! And Tex and the Crowells are goin' to expect us to join in with them."

"You're not goin' to, are you, Pa?" Samuel asked, knowing what the answer would be.

"No," Elijah answered thoughtfully. "We aren't goin' to, but you know what that means, don't you? Our neighbors are goin' to turn on us like we're poison. They won't want to have anything to do with us from now on."

"Are you sure?" Hannah asked. She was scarcely able to mouth the words.

"If you can believe what they say, I'm sure. That's what Tex followed me outside to tell me when I left his house a little while ago. If we don't go out and help 'em 'teach Standing Bear a lesson,' as they called it, we're no friends of theirs. He said they'd look on us as worse than the Indians!"

Red Terrence winced. He didn't know too much about living like a Christian yet. Situations like this made it hard for him.

"What're we goin' to do, Pa?" Samuel asked again.

Elijah dropped heavily to a chair at the kitchen table. "I've been prayin' and prayin' about it ever since I left Borman's place. The only thing I can think of is for us to go out into the willows along the river and do a real job of lookin' for those cattle. We've got to do our best to find 'em before Tex and the Crowells take out after Standing Bear!"

Samuel's stomach twisted painfully. He had been out since early morning looking for their cattle and oxen without finding them. And the way Tex and Amos sounded, they had been doing the same. What made his pa think they could find them now? And especially before Tex Borman decided to act?

Chapter 11

The Big Search

An hour before daylight Elijah got Samuel and Red out of bed. The boys had breakfast by the light of the coal-oil lamp and prayed with Mr. Prescott before saddling their horses.

"I'd like to go with you," Samuel's pa said, "but there are some things around the place I just have to take care of. You know how important this is, don't you?"

The boys nodded. "We've got to find those cattle before Mr. Borman and the Crowell brothers do something foolish—like going after Standing Bear with their rifles."

"That's not all," Elijah added. "We can manage without the cattle, somehow, but we need those oxen to plow the ground so we can plant our crops in the spring. Our saddle horses are too light to pull a plow through sod like this." He paused and breathed deeply. "We've got to have the oxen back, or we're in big trouble!"

Samuel Prescott shuddered. He knew his pa well. Elijah wouldn't talk this way if he weren't deeply disturbed. The boy was praying silently for guidance as he mounted his pony and followed Red across the firebreak.

Although they didn't voice their fears to each other, neither of the boys thought they had much chance of finding the cattle. There had been too much searching for the livestock earlier. Surely they would have been located if they were anywhere around.

Red and Samuel made their way across the blackened prairie to the place where there was grass again. The first faint gray wisps of morning were lighting the distant sky, and the early morning breeze was beginning to tease the tall grass. Finally, Samuel could stand it no longer.

"You don't suppose Standing Bear's men did take them, do you, Red?" he asked.

For a time before answering the older boy stood in the stirrups and stared at the hills across the river.

"Tex Borman swears that's what happened."

"I know it sounds that way, but I don't think Standing Bear would do that to us. You heard what he told Pa. He promised him that neither he nor his men would bother us. And you know he's a man who keeps his word."

"Maybe he didn't know they belonged to us. After the prairie fire we had to move them quite a ways from our buildings so they'd have grass to eat."

Samuel had been thinking about that possibility. He knew his pa didn't believe Standing Bear would break his word. If the Indian braves had taken the cattle, there had to be some reason for it. But what could it be? It was all a jumble to him.

Samuel and Red rode on for an hour or more, exploring every patch of willows along the river but without success. The sun had climbed over the

98

hills and was beginning to bring the sweat to Samuel's forehead. It was going to be another stifling day, he decided, pushing his hat back on his head and wiping the sweat away.

Red had gone on ahead. Samuel was about to kick his pony in the flanks and catch up with his friend when he saw a thin spiral of gray smoke twisting up against the sky from somewhere beyond the second ridge. At first fear seized him. Then he realized it was not another grass fire.

"See that?" he asked his companion.

"Must be that Indian hunting party that's following the buffalo herd."

That would mean the buffalo were over that way too. He would have liked to go over and see them. According to what everyone said, it was the biggest herd to come into their area in several years. But he knew what his pa would say if he and Red stopped searching for the cattle to take a look at the buffalo. Besides, the Indians were over that way.

They turned their horses and rode into the trees along the river in a desperate attempt to find the cattle. But it was as though one of the many ravines had suddenly opened up, swallowing them. They saw nothing that would indicate that the livestock had even been there.

Half an hour or so later they came out of the willows, onto the river bank and sat for a moment or two, looking beyond the stream to the hills on the other side of the valley. Red was the first to see the riders galloping up the steep slope. There were five or six white men heading in the direction of the Indian campfires. They were too far away for the boys to recognize either the men or their horses, but they didn't have to.

"Tex Borman!" Red exclaimed.

Samuel nodded. It was Tex, all right. It had to be! And he was heading straight for the Indian camp!

"Do you suppose Pa's with 'em?" he asked fearfully.

"You know better than that," Red Terrence replied. "Your pa wouldn't have any part in whatever it is those guys are fixin' to do."

Samuel faced his companion, the color leaving his ruddy cheeks.

"What're we goin' to do?"

Red shook his head. "You know what Borman's like when he's mad, and he's plenty mad about losin' all his cattle and his oxen. There isn't anything the two of us can do to stop him and his friends, that's for sure."

Samuel had to admit that Red was right. Tex and the Crowells and their two hired hands were determined to confront Standing Bear about stealing their stock. Nothing he and Red could do would stop them.

"I wish Pa were here," Samuel muttered under his breath. "I'll bet he'd stop 'em somehow."

Red's eyes lighted. "That's our only chance!"

Samuel didn't understand what he meant and said so.

"I'll ride back and get your pa!"

"I'll go with you!"

"My horse is faster than yours. Wait for me, Samuel! We'll get back just as fast as we can!" With that the older boy whirled his mount and went crashing through the willows in the direction of the Prescott place.

Samuel watched him disappear into the brush but made no attempt to follow him. What Red said was true. He would only hold him back. Young Prescott dismounted and led his horse down to the river to let him drink. He tried to figure out how long it would take Red to get his pa and get back. He and his friend had been gone from home for several hours, but they had been riding slowly and had taken the time to look everywhere the cattle could possibly have gone. In an hour or a little more Red and his pa should be on the other side of the river, getting close to the Indian hunting camp.

Then Samuel realized that he hadn't made arrangements to meet Red and his pa at any particular place. That meant he wouldn't be able to go to the Indian camp with them! And they might need him! There was only one thing he could do! He had to get to one of the hills where he would be high enough to see them and to be seen himself!

As soon as his horse had finished drinking, he mounted and urged his wiry young mare through the shallow water and up the bank on the other side. Excitement tingled up his spine as he urged his mount forward. He was praying silently with every step up the steep trail, asking God to restrain Tex Borman and his friends, to keep them from doing anything rash before his pa got there to stop them.

At the crest of the hill he looked toward the area where they had last seen the group of riders. There was no sign of them now. They had been riding hard and might have reached the Indian camp already. Samuel had to fight against the panic that welled up within him. If only he and Red had seen the settlers earlier, they would have had more time to get help!

"Dear God," he prayed, "just keep them from hurting anybody. Help them to understand that Standing Bear wouldn't steal from them!"

When he had finished praying, he started to ride again. Soon he realized that he was quite close to the herd of buffalo. He could hear their lowing and could see dust drifting lazily upward. Curious, he urged his horse in that direction.

A moment later he caught his breath sharply. In the valley below him, stretching for several miles in either direction, grazed more buffalo than he thought could possibly live in all the world. It was one great, moving mass of brown, like a river of animals. For the space of a minute or two he stared down at the great herd. Seeing so many buffalo in one place was awe inspiring. He could scarcely believe what he was seeing. No wonder the Indian people followed the huge buffalo herds. Meat and hides were always there for the taking. As long as they kept within hunting distance of the buffalo, they did not have to worry about going hungry.

Then he saw a dusty white animal, feeding among the broad, brown animals. He looked casually at it at first, seeing it without really looking at it. He had turned in the saddle and was looking in the opposite direction when he realized, suddenly, that he had seen something strange. His gaze whipped back, searching for it again.

This time his eyes found the animal and another like it nearby. Both animals were smaller than the buffalo and so decidedly different in color that they shouted for attention. It could be an albino buffalo, he reasoned. He had heard about them since coming west. Red said the albinos were often worshiped by the Indian people because of their strange color. They were thought to have a special and very powerful spirit.

The way he had heard it, though, the albinos were different from other buffalo only in color. He thought the albinos were about the same size as the others. But these animals were considerably smaller. In fact, there was something quite familiar about them.

It could be, he thought before checking himself. No, he dare not allow himself to speculate about the light-colored animals mixed with the dark buffalo. He had to get closer first to make sure.

Touching his horse in the flanks with his heels, he started down the slope in the general direction of the herd. He had to be careful about getting too close. All the men who told stories about their hunting experiences mentioned the difficulties they had when the powerful buffalo stampeded. Apparently, it didn't take much to excite them. So he approached the herd with care.

He got within a hundred yards or so and reined in hesitantly. His eyes widened. He had been right! Those light-colored animals weren't albino buffalo at all. They were oxen! What's more, they were his pa's oxen! That was the reason they looked so familiar. He had yoked and unyoked them so many times he had lost count, and he had sat behind them for so many miles he could have counted the hairs on their broad sides.

But what were they doing with the buffalo? He had never heard of anything like that before!

If his pa's oxen were running with the buffalo, he reasoned, what about the other oxen and cattle? Maybe they had joined the big herd too.

He rode along the edge of the herd, staying just far enough away to keep from disturbing them. A few minutes later he saw three or four cows and another pair of oxen. He was trembling with excitement.

Standing Bear hadn't stolen the livestock at all! They had mixed with the buffalo herd on their own. Relief washed over him in great, healing waves. And then his lean body stiffened.

Tex Borman and the Crowells didn't know where their cattle were! They thought the Indian chief had stolen them! Even now they might be causing big trouble!

Chapter 12

Trouble at the Indian Camp

Samuel glanced up at the blazing sun. He didn't know why, but it seemed that the sun was racing across the broad, cloudless sky. And still his pa and Red weren't back. If they didn't make it soon, it would be too late! Even if they did get to the Indian hunting camp in time to stop Tex Borman and his friends, his pa might have trouble getting the hotheaded Texan to listen to reason. Pa didn't even know about the cattle being with the herd of buffalo! He was the one who knew that!

Suddenly Samuel realized what he had to do! He had the information that could stop a fight! He couldn't afford to wait until Red and his pa came along! He had to get to the Indian camp right away! Even now it might be too late!

Leaning forward in the saddle, Samuel urged his surefooted saddle pony into a hard gallop. He guided her up the hill, along the grass-shrouded ridge and into a shallow valley between the hills. The Indian hunting camp was not in sight, but that did not disturb the 13 year old. Samuel knew the camp would be just beyond the crest of the next hill in a place where the braves could command a close view of all the approaches to it. Seldom did they choose a campsite that did not give them the protection of being able to see the surrounding area.

After running his horse for a time, Samuel reined her in to a walk to let her rest. When he started on, he held her to a fast trot. At that speed she would be able to keep going for a long time, even on such a blistering day. One of the first things his pa had taught him about horses was to take good care of them and especially not to run them too hard. So, though he was impatient, he was careful not to push his pony beyond her endurance. But it seemed to take forever to get within sight of the Indian hunting camp. He rode up to the crest of the next hill and saw the tepees, pitched just beyond the highest point of ground.

And there was Tex Borman! He and his friends had ridden to the edge of the camp and were astride their horses, faced by several frightened women and two or three old men.

"I'm tellin' you for the last time!" Tex grated. "You're goin' to have to pay up for the cattle you killed or we aren't responsible for what happens to you!"

"They don't understand what you're sayin', Tex," Amos Crowell observed quietly. "They don't understand a word of it."

"Don't you believe it! Those lyin' rascals just don't want to understand, that's all."

Samuel rode forward hurriedly, pushing his mount between the Indian people and Tex Borman and his friends.

"Get that nag of yours out of the way!" Tex blustered, swearing. "Just what do you think you're doin', anyway?"

"I found the cattle, Mr. Borman!" Samuel blurted excitedly.

"So did we. What's left of 'em!" His face was white with anger. "Right here in this camp just like I said we would!"

"That can't be! I just saw 'em with that big herd of buffalo! You can come with me and see for yourself!" He held out his hand appealingly.

Borman didn't even hear him.

"You had a bell on that lead cow of yours, didn't you? Well, look what that kid's playin' with. Now maybe you and that stubborn pa of yours will believe what I'm tellin' you!"

Samuel stared down at the cowbell a boy of seven or eight was playing with. There was no doubt about it—it was the bell his pa had put on Elizabeth, their best cow. One of their neighbors back in Illinois had made it for them. There could be no mistake about it. There wouldn't be another cowbell like that one for many miles.

"Maybe it fell off Elizabeth, and he found it," he said lamely.

Borman snorted. "Maybe that cowhide over there on the stretcher fell off of her too!"

There was no doubt about the hide. It had come from their cow, just as the bell had.

"M-maybe she died, and—and they took off the bell and skinned her to get the hide," he said, knowing his reasoning was weak, even as he spoke.

Tex laughed as he shook his head.

"You sure don't give up easily, do you, kid?" Amos asked. "Why are you stickin' up for 'em this way?"

"You know why!" Borman blurted. "You heard what his pa said when we wanted him to

107

come along with us, didn't you? The whole bunch has got jelly where their backbones ought to be!"

"I know where the rest of the cattle and the oxen are," Samuel persisted, ignoring the taunting in the Texan's voice. "Just come with me, and I'll show you!"

"I didn't think you'd lie, kid," Tex continued. "You and that family of yours are such good Christians!"

Amos glanced up at the sun. "Time's wastin', Tex. Let's get this business over with and get out of here before those bloodthirsty braves get back!"

Borman spurred his horse and rode forward, pushing Samuel's saddle pony out of the way. The belligerent man glared down at the Indian people who were still standing there helplessly.

"I'm goin' to give you one more chance!" he snarled. "Come across with pay for our cattle, or we'll take enough of your ponies to pay for 'em! Understand?"

At that instant Elijah Prescott and Red Terrence came dashing up on their lathered mounts. They obviously hadn't spared their saddle horses in the frantic ride to the Indian camp.

Seeing Samuel's father was unsettling to Borman for a moment or two. He shifted nervously in his saddle. "I thought you said you didn't want any part of this!"

"That's right! I don't want any part of what you've been plannin'." Elijah looked at his son and down at the women and old men who were blocking the path into the camp. "What's goin' on here?"

"Just what I said was goin' on when I last talked to you. I came over here with Amos and

108

Aaron and their men to get pay for the cattle this bunch of thieves stole."

"But they didn't steal the cattle, Pa!" Samuel blurted out. "I found 'em mixed in with the buffalo a little while ago."

Elijah's eyes brightened. "I don't know why I didn't think of that. I've heard of cattle and oxen wanderin' off with the buffalo, but I never once figured that happened to us." He turned to Borman. "Come on, Tex. Let's go over and see if we can figure some way of separatin' 'em. How about it?"

"It's not quite as simple as that," the Texan said. "I'm not sure what that boy of yours is tryin' to pull, but I know for a fact that he's lyin'." He pointed out the cowbell and the stretched hide. "I don't know why I'm gettin' so riled up about this. It's your cow that was killed."

"That's right," Elijah said sternly. "It's my cow that was killed. And there's something else I want you to know. If Samuel says he saw our cattle and oxen mixed in with the buffalo, that's exactly what he saw. He doesn't lie!"

Tex glared at Elijah. "There's been enough of this foolishness," he snarled. "Get out of my way!"

Mr. Prescott did not move.

"Get out of my way, I tell you!"

"What are you goin' to do?"

"I'm goin' over and take enough of their ponies to pay for the cattle we lost."

Elijah shook his head. "I don't think that'd be wise, Tex," he said quietly.

"And what makes you so sure about that?"

"If you take those ponies, Standing Bear will

109

be on your trail before you've had time to get home. He'll make you pay double for every animal of his you take."

"Listen, Prescott," Borman said, his tone changing. "How many times do I have to tell you? The only thing these savages respect is force! Treat 'em rough, and they'll know better than to mess around with us the next time. Let 'em think we're afraid of 'em, and they'll run us clear out of the country."

There was a long silence.

"So move aside, Prescott, and let us get on with our business here. I don't want to have trouble with you too."

"But I'm afraid you do have trouble with us, Borman."

"Just what do you mean by that?"

"I mean we're not goin' to let you take any of Standing Bear's horses."

Tex Borman could not believe what he had just heard. "Do you mean to tell us you're sidin' with these filthy Indians instead of with us?"

"You can call it anything you want to, Tex, but I can't let you do it."

He fingered the butt of his revolver. "I wouldn't want to have to use this on you, Elijah. I've never shot a man before."

Still Mr. Prescott did not back away. "You're goin' to have to use it, Tex, if you do what you say you're goin' to. I'm just not goin' to let you do it!"

For the space of half a minute the two men stared at each other. Then Tex's gaze lowered, slowly.

"I never thought I'd live to see the day when a white man would side with the Indians against

110

me." He shook his head. "We're neighbors, Elijah, but I can tell you right now, as far as Nellie and I are concerned, you don't live out here anymore!"

"I'm sorry you feel that way, Tex, but there are times when a man has to do what's right."

Samuel was so proud of his pa, he could hardly stand it. There weren't very many men who would have the courage to stand against five armed men because he believed they weren't doing what was right and honest.

Tex Borman turned his horse slowly and started to ride away. His companions followed him. But they had only gone a dozen steps when they heard a chilling war scream, and two dozen warriors led by Standing Bear came charging into the camp. Stunned momentarily, Tex reined in. An instant later they were ringed by warriors.

Rage twisted Standing Bear's face until Samuel could scarcely recognize him. He rode up close to Borman, and his powerful hand reached out and caught the Texan by the shirt collar, almost jerking him off his horse.

"You! What you come here for? You sneak in like a coyote and bluster before the children and women and old men! Why you come here?"

"Standing Bear," Elijah broke in quickly, "let me explain!"

"I do not want to hear from your lips, my friend! I want to hear from this one! This one who frightens the women and the children and is so brave before the old ones whose strength has gone."

"It was all a misunderstanding, Chief," Elijah persisted. "I can—"

111

"I will speak to you when I want words from you. Be quiet and remain my friend!"

Samuel shuddered. He was more afraid now than he had ever been in his life. He had never seen Standing Bear half so angry. Tex and his companions were frightened too. Their faces were white and lined with sweat, and their hands trembled.

Chapter 13

The Stampede

Tex Borman moistened his lips and stared helplessly at Elijah. His eyes pleaded with the older man to do something to help him.

"Speak!" Standing Bear rasped. "Tell us how a rabbit has the courage of a bear. You are a brave one, White Man. You face women and old men with no strings on their bows. Tell us! *Tell us!*"

"It—it's like Elijah said," Tex stammered. He was pleading now—pleading for his life. "It's all a mistake. You see, we thought you had stolen our cattle, but when we came over here to talk about it, you were gone, so we thought we would talk with the old men about it—to see what they knew. But we weren't goin' to hurt anyone. And that's a fact. When we saw that you had only skinned one cow, we decided there must be some good explanation so we—we were goin' to leave. Isn't that right?" He glanced at the men who had ridden into the camp with him. They nodded vigorously.

The Indian chief tightened his grip on the frightened young man. "Put your forked tongue away, White Man. We saw you come this way. We followed you here. You were going to take our ponies—a pony for a cow. But you not wait until you know if we had stolen your cattle. You decided we had. And you came to steal our horses to pay for them."

Borman licked his lips. "That's not the way it was," he protested. "We weren't goin' to do harm to anyone. Honest we weren't."

"Your words are as crooked as a small boy's arrow." Standing Bear hauled Tex even closer to him. Their faces were only inches apart. "You owe my friend and his son much this day. If not for them and what they did to stop you, your scalps would be on our belts by this time."

Borman jerked convulsively.

"Remember that next time you try to frighten an Indian's women and children and old men." He shoved Tex back into the saddle so violently that the young man had to grab the horn to right himself. "Now leave! And do not come back here! Any of you! You are not welcome in Standing Bear's camp!"

The Texan muttered darkly under his breath, whirled his horse and galloped away. His companions followed him. Once they were gone, Standing Bear turned to Elijah and the boys. "Come to my tepee. There is much I want to talk to you about."

They did as he asked them to. When they were inside the chief's tepee, sitting cross-legged opposite him, he explained about killing the cow. When the hunters went out, some of the boys went along. It was their custom to ride with the hunters on the chase. No one expected them to kill a buffalo. They went so they would get used to the herd and learn how to cut out one buffalo and ride alongside of him long enough to shoot an arrow at

114

him. The cattle had run with the herd, but they could not keep up. Standing Bear still did not know how he had done it, but one of the boys had managed to kill the cow.

"We did not know she belonged to you, my friend," the chief said. "We thought she belonged to one of our enemies, so we skinned her. Now I want to talk to you about paying for the cow."

"I could not take anything for her, Standing Bear. Let us say I give her to you as one friend to another."

The stately Sioux pulled himself erect, and his face darkened. "Would you deny me the honor of making what I say to you straight and true as the course of the sun through the sky? I will pay for the cow!"

Elijah and the boys saw that it would not be wise to insist that the cow be a gift.

"Is it possible for you to help us get the cattle and oxen separated from the herd of buffalo?" Elijah asked. "If it is, you could more than repay us for the cow by helping us get our livestock back."

Standing Bear was silent for a moment. "They do not run as fast as the buffalo," he said, "and we are going hunting after we eat. That's where we started when we saw those white men riding toward our camp and followed them back here. Yes, my friend, we will help you get your animals away from the buffalo herd. Is that all you want for the cow we killed?"

"All?" Elijah echoed. "It is far more than enough. Without your help, they are all gone." He and the boys could try to run the herd and get the livestock separated from the buffalo, but he wasn't

115

sure there were enough of them to do it. One thing he did not want to do was bring Tex and the others over to help. If the Indians happened to be there, he would just be creating one more opportunity for trouble. "If you help us get the rest of our stock back, you will have paid for the cow three times over."

After a meal of buffalo meat Standing Bear and his warriors went back to the place where the herd was grazing. Mr. Prescott, his son and Red Terrence went along.

"We're not to get involved in chasing the buffalo," Elijah explained to the boys. "Standing Bear and his men will take care of that. They'll get the herd running hard enough to outstrip the cattle. When that happens, we're to ride between the cattle and the buffalo and cut them off."

"Sounds good," Samuel observed.

"If we can only pull it off," Red put in.

Standing Bear had Elijah, Samuel and Red station themselves about half a mile ahead of the place where the cattle and buffalo were grazing.

"When they get this far, they will be behind the slowest buffalo. Then you take them from the herd," the Indian said.

It seemed to Samuel that it took the Indians forever to get started. They went some distance behind the buffalo and worked themselves carefully into position. Then, with a triumphant whoop, they charged the buffalo. For a few moments all was confusion. The buffalo milled about in fright, jostling into each other in their haste to get away from the screeching horsemen. Once the herd started moving, however, they charged headlong up the valley.

116

"Look!" Red cried. "Did you ever see anything like it?"

Seeing the stampede was even more awesome than looking at the herd as it grazed. The cumbersome animals drew on a strength and speed Samuel didn't know they had. The ground shook beneath their thundering hooves.

The chase worked out exactly as Standing Bear had said it would. The buffalo could run almost twice as fast as the oxen and cattle. Before the herd had moved a quarter of a mile, the tame livestock were badly outdistanced. All Elijah and the boys had to do was ride between the lumbering stock and the buffalo. Turning back the oxen and cattle was no problem at all. Long before the buffalo quit running, the settlers had turned their small herd and were moving them slowly up the hill.

"We got 'em!" Samuel said exultantly. "We don't have to worry about how we're goin' to get our plowin' done now."

When they were two or three miles away from the buffalo herd, Elijah had Samuel ride ahead to get Tex Borman and the Crowells to help them divide the stock and keep them separated.

"What if he doesn't believe me when I tell him we've got 'em?" the boy asked.

"He'll believe you."

"He didn't this mornin' when I tried to tell him I'd found 'em."

"If he doesn't believe you, tell him to come anyway," Elijah said. "That way he'll find out you're tellin' the truth."

It took Samuel a little longer to get the other settlers than he figured it would. His pa and Red

117

were within a mile of the house when he and Tex Borman and the others finally met them.

"You did have the cattle!" Tex exclaimed, pushing his hat back on his head and scratching his ear. "I thought for a minute or two that you might be funnin' me."

"We'd have brought 'em over to you, but we didn't figure we could manage separatin' 'em, even if we did know for sure who owned what."

Tex was scarcely listening to him. "How'd you manage it?" he wanted to know. "How'd you get that evil scoundrel to turn 'em loose?"

"You mean Standing Bear?" Elijah asked. "Like Samuel tried to tell you, he didn't have 'em."

The Texan's eyes narrowed suspiciously. "Now don't give me that!"

"I'm tellin' you the truth. Standing Bear didn't have our stock. They'd wandered into the buffalo herd and took up with 'em, that's all."

Borman knew that sort of thing did happen. He had seen it himself when he was riding trail from Texas. "But if that happened, how'd you get your hands on 'em again?"

"You might have a little trouble believin' this, but it's the truth too: Standing Bear and his men helped us."

Amos Crowell gasped. "That murderer?"

"He's a fine gentleman," Elijah countered, "and an honorable man. He insisted on paying for the cow they had killed, so I asked him to have his men help us get our stock back. They ran the herd, and when the cattle lagged behind, we cut 'em off. It was as simple as that."

118

Borman shook his head. "I swear," he muttered under his breath. "I swear!"

"God sure answered our prayers," Elijah said thankfully.

Tex Borman eyed him curiously. "I've been doin' a lot of serious thinkin' lately—ever since my wife . . . ever since she got to talkin' to Hannah. I want to come over and see you one of these days and—" He glanced in the direction of Amos Crowell and felt the color come up in his cheeks. "Is that all right?"

"Sure thing. How about tonight?"

"Sounds fine. We'll be over right after supper."

"I thought we were goin' to play some cribbage, Tex," Amos protested.

"Yeah, that's right. We were goin' to play some cribbage tonight, but it'll have to wait. I'm fixin' to see Elijah tonight."

At first Samuel didn't know for sure what the Texan wanted to talk to his pa about. Then he caught that knowing look in Tex's eyes. He knew then what the conversation was to be about. He knew as well that there would be a lot of prayer for Mr. Borman at the Prescott home before he and his wife, Nellie, arrived. She was a Christian. He was sure that, after tonight, Tex would be a believer too.

*   *   *

" 'Dear Diary,

" 'That's how we came to settle in what's now northwestern Nebraska. We never did get all the way out to Oregon.

" 'We all thought Standing Bear was going to become a Christian, but he didn't. I'm writing this last note about ten years after we first settled on this land and built our little sod house. Standing Bear died and was buried yesterday. Pa had been over to talk to him about Jesus Christ several times, but he couldn't see that salvation was for him.

" 'But there are some Christians among the Indians who live around here. Gray Thunder—the one who liked my cookies so well he wanted to buy me—was the first. Then two of Standing Bear's sons received Christ. We are praying there will be more.

" 'Good-bye, dear diary. I haven't treated you very well lately, but now all of your pages are full. It makes me happy to read again about what happened to us on the way out here and how God took care of us every step of the way.

" 'All my love,
" 'Becky.' "

There were tears in Trena's eyes when she finished reading and closed the little book. "Here," she said, holding it out to Grandma Redding.

The old woman refused to take it, however. "Keep it, my dear. You may have a little girl of your own someday. If you do, I'm sure she'll want to read Becky's story."

by Bernard Palmer

THE BRADLEYS AND THE MYSTERIOUS LETTER   6251-X

Jonathan Bradley and his family of four children move to a small midwest town. They decide to purchase a run-down farm on the outskirts of Collinsdale. Shortly after moving in they begin receiving threatening letters demanding that they sell the farm. A masked face at a window, the barn mysteriously set on fire, a furtive old woman at a local hotel—all these add to the suspense and eventually to a happy conclusion.

THE BRADLEYS AND THE NEW SKIS   6252-8

Tim Bradley befriends Bill, a frightened and often defensive neighbor boy who lives with a gruff and cruel uncle, a horse and a ferocious dog. Tim is puzzled by the apparent discrepancies in Bill's stories, disturbed by the suggestion that Bill's beautiful ski outfit and expensive skis may have been stolen, and appalled by the dilemma he faces because of his friendship with Bill.

TRENA AND THE OLD DIARY   6253-6

Locked in the pages of an ancient diary Trena finds a covered-wagon adventure, complete with the antagonism of the wagon train leaders, disabled wagons and the constant threat of Indian attack. Becky and Samuel Prescott, Trena's friends from the past, are left behind by the wagon train with their parents. There they discover a sick and injured Indian boy and nurse him back to health, only to face the wrath of his warrier father who accuses them of kidnapping.

HOMESTEADING IN STANDING BEAR'S TERRITORY   6254-4

Trena's friends from the past, Becky and Samuel Prescott, step once again from the pages of the old diary and live their exciting adventures while homesteading in the old west. When the Indian scouts desert the wagon train to search for gold, the Prescotts are forced to abandon the trip to Oregon and settle in Indian territory. There they encounter Standing Bear and his braves, battle a forest fire and solve the mystery of the missing cattle herd.

JON AND THE BREAK-IN MYSTERY   6255-2

Jon had no idea how much trouble he would get involved in when he decided to keep and train goats as a do-it-yourself, money-making project. His friendship with Marv and partnership in a concession venture at the fall festival brought his problems to a climax. Accused of shoplifting and of breaking into the school, Jon eventually gets his name cleared in an unexpected way.

Each book—75¢

Back to the Bible Broadcast
Box 82808, Lincoln, Nebraska 68501 or
Box 10, Winnipeg, Manitoba R3C 2G2